D0625925

SWITCH UP

STRIPES PUBLISHING LIMITED
An imprint of the Little Tiger Group
1 Coda Studios, 189 Munster Road, London SW6 6AW

A paperback original
First published in Great Britain in 2019

ISBN: 978-1-78895-040-4

Printed and bound in the UK.

10 9 8 7 6 5 4 3 2 1

THE SWITCH UP

KATY CANNON

Stripes

WILLA

I am an expert in parent behaviour. After watching mine for the last fourteen years, I've learned all the tricks they use to control us. And over the last six months, I think my mum and dad have tried *all* of them. (Fortunately, my expert status means I'm also *excellent* at counter-attack. I know all the best ways to exact revenge … like my recent shopping spree. With Mum's credit card.)

The number one thing I've learned is: parents always *say* they're doing what's best for you, when really, they're doing what's best for *them*.

"I don't know why you're being so difficult about this." Mum sighed. I risked a glance across at her, and saw her 'I'm so misunderstood' look had settled firmly in place. Trick number twenty-seven – make your offspring feel sorry for you. "When I was your age I'd have *loved* to spend a summer in Italy. So romantic!"

"So remote," I countered. She wasn't getting any agreement from me this week. On anything.

Besides, I totally wasn't buying her 'Italy – land of romance' line. She was just using trick forty-two: trying to make herself feel less guilty for sending me away by pretending that she'd love the chance to go.

I knew the truth. My summer wasn't going to be like that movie Mum loved, with Audrey Hepburn. There'd be no whizzing around Rome on a Vespa or whatever.

Instead, my parents, in a shocking show of actual communication and co-operation with each other, had agreed to ship me off to some random relative. I'll admit, I'd been too busy sulking to really listen to the details, but I'd definitely heard enough to be sure of the following:

1. The aunt lived on a farm.

2. The farm was in the middle of nowhere, Italy.

3. Italy wasn't London, where I was *supposed* to be spending the summer.

I'd had it all planned. Mum had even agreed! Well, eventually, anyway.

We were supposed to be flying back from LA together at the beginning of August, once her guest role on this US TV show had finished filming. I'd been out there with her ever since my school broke up (at the start of July – perk of the private school Dad insisted I went to. The long holidays *almost* made up for the awful uniform.)

She was going to hand me over to Dad, and we were going to spend summer in the city together, as an adventure. It would be my first time seeing him since he and Mum officially split up, over a month ago, and Dad disappeared to London to appear in some theatre show while he was on sabbatical from the TV soap he stars in, *Heatherside*. We'd even arranged for me to attend a course at a London theatre, which was a *huge* deal. I'd been nagging them to let me follow them both into the business, ever since I turned eleven, three whole years ago. But they both said that show business was no place for their child.

I'd hoped, when they agreed to me taking the course, that they were *finally* accepting that I wasn't a child any more. How wrong could I be?

I'd heard about the course from one of my dad's co-stars on *Heatherside*. Apparently, it was *the* course to do if you were serious about getting into TV acting – especially since they always got a casting agent to come along to the final showcase. And since Mum and Dad insisted on me going to a boring private school instead of stage school, it was my best shot at getting into the industry. So I'd found the website, registered myself using my own email, got Mum to sign the parental consent form and sent it in.

But then the show Dad had a part in down in London got picked as a last-minute replacement for some cancelled act at the Edinburgh Fringe Festival, and Mum's US TV series guest role got extended into a regular part with longer filming hours, and suddenly everything changed. London was totally off the cards – even though my parents *knew* how much I wanted to do my theatre course.

Clearly, Dad had other priorities now, besides his only daughter. He didn't want me in Edinburgh with him – said he would be too busy to look after me. And Mum's new role was more important to her than anything *I* wanted.

Even so, staying with Mum might have been OK. I mean, summer in California isn't exactly a punishment, right? But it turned out I wouldn't be in LA. Nor would I be with Dad in Edinburgh. And I certainly wouldn't be in London attending the theatre course. Instead, I was being sent to Italy, to stay with the random aunt.

Honestly, it was enough to make me Google 'how to divorce your parents'. (Which I had done. Several times. LA was clearly rubbing off on me.)

Even if I'd had to give up my plans for London, I'd had opportunities in LA – enough that the summer might not have been a total bust in terms of kick-starting my acting career. The TV show Mum worked on had a day off from filming, and all the young stars and crew had been heading to the beach. They'd even invited me to join them – my first real chance at networking.

But was I on the beach? No. I was in a car with the air conditioning turned up way too high, pulling up at Los Angeles airport, ready for my flight to nowhere.

"So I'm going to leave you with the UM person from the airline, OK?" Mum said, obviously trying to sound like the kind of mother who cared about her daughter's wellbeing. Of course, if she *actually* cared, she wouldn't be making me go to Italy. (I'd pointed that out a few times the night before and Mum said I was being overdramatic. Coming from an actress that seemed kind of hypocritical.)

"UM?" I asked.

"Willa, we've been over this! The Unaccompanied Minors person!"

Ah, now she sounded like the exasperated Mum I knew and tolerated.

"Makes me sound like one of those stupid classical

music pieces Dad pretends to like," I muttered. If anyone else was within earshot, Dad always had classical music playing. The rest of the time it was eighties pop all the way. Just hearing Wham! made me miss him.

Mum ignored me. As usual. "The UM person will look after you until your Aunt Sofia meets you in London. Then you'll travel together to her place in Italy."

Aunt Sofia. A woman I'd never met and knew next to nothing about, who was probably as annoyed about the arrangement as I was. Although apparently she had foster kids staying with her, so an extra person wouldn't make much difference. (One was about my age, but I was guessing they were the oldest. I really hoped she wasn't going to expect me to help out with the others. I'm not good with little kids.)

Still, it wasn't Aunt Sofia's fault I had to go stay with her on a farm miles away from any sort of entertainment or decent shopping, in a country where I didn't speak the language. I was sure Aunt Sofia was a perfectly lovely person.

Unlike my parents.

"Right." Grabbing my leather jacket from the seat beside me, I opened the car door and stepped out on to the baking hot pavement. I could feel the heat seeping through my flip-flops.

It wasn't until Mum got out, though, that I saw the photographer.

"Sarra! Sarra!" he called out. "Over here, Sarra. How about a smile?"

Mum gave a polite smile for the camera, then put up her hand as a shield so he couldn't get any photos of her pulling funny faces. The number of paparazzi trying to get her photo after the news broke about Dad, a month or so ago, had taught her that trick pretty quickly.

"Have you spoken to Scott, Sarra?" the photographer called out, and Mum and I both froze.

Scott is my dad, in case you haven't guessed.

"How did you find out about his new girlfriend?" the photographer yelled, happily sharing my family's private business with everyone taking a plane out of LA that day. But his question shook us out of our stunned state, and Mum grabbed my arm to pull me towards the back of the cab, where the driver was unloading my case from the boot.

"Did he tell you himself?" the photographer continued.

I knew the answer to that one: no. Mum found

out the same way I did. The same way most of the country did – when photos of Dad and his co-star kissing showed up in the papers.

I wasn't telling the paparazzi that, though. Rule one of being a celebrity's daughter – don't tell the press anything. And I wasn't just *a* celebrity's daughter. I was Willa Andrews, daughter of Scott and Sarra Andrews, the darlings of British TV. Or they had been, until this year.

Now I was Willa Andrews, unwanted daughter of two feuding celebs who were too busy dealing with the fallout from their own stupidity to care about me.

Not that I was bitter or anything.

"Sarra! How about a photo with your friend, then?"

Obviously a newbie, if he didn't recognize me as Mum's daughter. Mind you, that would make Mum's new LA agent, Veronica, happy. According to *her* I wasn't helping my mother's flourishing career one bit.

"Let's get inside, Willa," Mum said through her teeth.

Taking my suitcase from the driver, I followed Mum through the automatic doors and into the terminal.

LAX was bustling, as always. Mum stopped when we were far enough away from the doors and switched back from celeb mode to mum mode. "Now, have you got everything you need?"

"Hope so," I said, shrugging on my jacket. I figured if I'd forgotten anything, I'd just have to buy it when I got there. On Mum's credit card, of course. Assuming she'd unblocked it after my shopping spree last week, anyway.

Mum frowned at me, then smoothed out her expression again. I could almost hear her thinking 'wrinkles' as she did it.

"Do you really need to take that jacket?" she asked. "It's worth a fortune and I don't want you leaving it somewhere. It'll be far too hot to wear it in Italy."

I wrapped my arms round myself inside the leather jacket, thankful for the air conditioning that meant I wasn't overheating. I *loved* my jacket. It was the one I'd worn for the magazine photo shoot Mum and I did right after we arrived in LA at the start of the summer. Before Veronica decided that having a teenage daughter wasn't good for Mum's image. Too aging, apparently, now she had this bigger role and the possibility of a part in the *next* series too.

I wasn't sure if Veronica had shared this insight with Mum, but she'd shared it with someone in a phone call that I just happened to overhear. (OK, fine, I was listening in.) "She could make it really big over here now she's dropped the deadweight husband. People love a survivor. The daughter's not helping, though. Too old to be passed off as cute. We'll have to come up with a strategy for that, if she wants roles as anything other than The Mother."

But that day at the magazine shoot – with us both in ripped jeans and matching leather jackets (hers was navy, mine was cherry red) – it had felt like Mum and me against the world. Against all the friends and papers talking about our family. Against Dad, and his midlife crisis.

I'd thought it could be the start of a whole new life for us.

Turns out I was wrong.

Mum sighed, again. One small win to me. I smirked.

"Come on, then. Let's get you on this flight."

My smirk disappeared. Six thousand miles' worth of wins to Mum.

ALICE

I've been called a lot of things over the last fourteen years. When I was little, my dad used to call me Starfish. Mum would use my full name whenever I was in trouble – *Alice Josephine Wright!* Not that I got into trouble often or anything, but I knew to come running when I heard it.

At school my friends had tried shortening my name all sorts of ways – Allie, Al, Liss, that sort of thing.

My teachers called me a dream pupil, top of the class, even best in school. (Apart from the PE teacher, who called me a hopeless case. She wasn't wrong.)

The counsellor I went to see after Mum died had some other names for me. An anxious child, that was the main one. Compulsive planner. Perfectionist. Afraid to disappoint. Avoids conflict.

But mostly, I was just Alice.

Today though, I'd gained a new name. One I *really* didn't like.

Unaccompanied Minor.

Even the words are rubbish.

Unaccompanied. Alone. Abandoned.

Minor. Yes, technically it just meant under eighteen. But it also meant unimportant.

Abandoned and unimportant, that was me. And stuck in the Los Angeles airport waiting for a connecting flight home.

Normally I liked airports. They were exciting – full of people beginning and ending adventures. But today I felt I'd much rather be at the beach, listening to the wind on the water and feeling the waves flow over my toes.

Before my mum died, we only used to go through airports for rare holidays abroad. But over the last four years I'd spent a lot more time in them, following my dad to wherever his latest research trip took him.

This summer he was working on his biggest project yet – helping out with marine biology research on the Great Barrier Reef. Flying out to Australia two weeks earlier, I hadn't cared about any of the other travel stories going on around me. I'd been too excited about spending time with my dad in such an amazing location.

Flying back without him was a different matter altogether.

Mandy the airline representative had met me off my

flight from Australia to Los Angeles (taking over from another woman called Fran) and was now in charge of me – and the other UMs, I supposed – until we boarded our next flight. As we walked away from the gate where I'd got off the plane, she gave me a small smile. I got the feeling that she wanted to pat me on the head like a little kid.

"Are you nervous about flying alone?" She sniffed, like she was coming down with a cold.

"Not really." What did she think I'd been doing between Australia and LA? Fran had checked in once or twice, but mostly it was just me and the snoring businessman beside me.

Many things in the world made me anxious or nervous, but I'd found it wasn't usually the ones that other people thought I should be worried about.

"Well, our Unaccompanied Minors scheme is here to support all our young flyers," Mandy went on, like she was reading aloud from her clipboard. "We've just got a little time before your flight to –" she checked – "London, so why don't we take a seat with some other UMs in our special lounge? Maybe you can make some new friends." There was no enthusiasm in her voice, but that was OK. I wasn't feeling very enthusiastic about it either.

The 'lounge' was a tiny room near one of the gates, adjacent to one of the proper business lounges. There were three other kids there – a girl about my age watching something on a tablet and two younger boys who were probably brothers. There was a table in the middle set out with bottles of water, soft drinks and some cookies.

"Here we go!" Mandy gestured to the room like it was the Taj Mahal. I smiled dutifully. "You make yourself at home now."

Then she sat down next to the door and pulled out her phone, jabbing the screen furiously. I guessed I was on my own again. Which, after hours of the snoring businessman, was actually kind of a relief.

I took a seat near the cookies and pulled a book out of my bag. But before I could get stuck into the story, there was an announcement over the tannoy. "Flight BA344 to London has been delayed." I groaned.

"Hey." The girl with the tablet pulled off her headphones – they were the big sort that go over your whole ears. "Was that the London flight?"

I nodded. "Delayed."

"Maybe someone should go and find out more about that," she said loudly, looking pointedly at Mandy.

Mandy didn't notice. The girl rolled her eyes and

shifted into the seat next to me. "You as bored as I am?"

"I just got here," I said. "But give me a minute."

She grinned. "I'm Willa," she said, then just stared at me. It took me a moment to realize she was waiting for me to give her my name.

"Alice."

"Hey, are you two twins?" the elder of the two boys asked, looking up at us across the table.

Willa and I exchanged a look, assessing each other's appearance. We both had dark hair, but her eyes were golden brown not green like mine, and she was a little taller too. Plus she definitely had a few more curves than me. I bet the boys at her school didn't tease her like the ones at my school did me.

But we did look alike. I mean, surprisingly alike. Face shape, hair, even her smile looked a bit like mine. I couldn't really blame the boy for asking.

Willa was less understanding.

"Obviously," Willa said. "We're totally twins. That's why we arrived at different times and *just* introduced ourselves to each other."

I hid a smile as the boy turned away, grumbling.

"So you're going to London as well?" she asked, and I nodded. "On holiday?"

"Sort of," I replied, waggling my head from side to side a little. "It's complicated."

"Tell me about it." Willa gave an overly dramatic sigh and switched off her tablet. "I *should* be spending the summer here in LA with my mum, or in Edinburgh with my dad."

"I was supposed to be staying with my dad in Australia for the summer, while he worked."

"Working in Australia? That's cool."

I smiled. It *was* cool. It was his dream, in fact. "Yeah. He's a Professor of Marine Biology."

Willa's eyes widened a little. Dad's job title sounded a lot more impressive if you hadn't met him.

"So what happened?" I asked. "Why are you heading to London?"

"I'm not," Willa replied, flicking her hair over her shoulder. "London would be perfect. London was the *original* plan, before my parents messed it up. But London is just where I'm being collected by an aunt I've never met. Then she's stealing me away to some farm in the middle of nowhere, Italy."

An Italian farmhouse. My mind filled with memories of our last family holiday before Mum died – a little cottage on the Italian coast, where we hung out on the beach all day, Mum resting on a lounger.

We spent our evenings eating huge bowls of pasta on the patio outside the cottage, stars twinkling overhead and Dad telling stories about them. Mum would doze off quite often, and then Dad would carry her to bed. But still, it was perfect.

Mum had wanted to tick the last item off her bucket list while we were there – visiting some waterfall near the coast that was supposed to have magical powers – but she hadn't been well enough to go in the end.

If I ever got to visit Italy again, that was where I was going. To the waterfall Mum said could take away all of your worries.

"Is it by the sea?" I asked.

Willa gave me a look. The sort of look my friends give me when I say something weird. Usually about marine life.

"I think so, yeah," she said. "I mean, I wasn't really listening when my mum was going on and on about how great it would be, but I think she said something about a beach. Probably a stupid rocky one you can't sunbathe on."

"Sounds pretty great to me," I admitted. "Although maybe that's just because it's anywhere but London."

"Are you crazy?" Willa asked. "London is the best! It has theatres and shops and the Harry Potter Studios and *everything*. I used to go there with my parents all the time before—" She cut herself off.

I didn't ask 'before what?' I'd done the same often enough when I found myself almost talking about Mum. Whatever Willa's *before* was, she didn't want to talk about it. Just like I tended to tell people it was only me and Dad these days, if they asked, and not elaborate on where my mum was.

"It's not London I don't like," I explained. "It's who I have to stay with."

"Worse than a random aunt?" Willa asked, eyebrows raised.

"Much. A random woman my dad used to work with who I've never met, know nothing about and who he hadn't even *mentioned* until he needed to get rid of me for the rest of the summer." And that wasn't even the worst part. The worst part was how he'd told me about her.

Willa looked taken aback at my sudden outburst. "Whoa. I guess I'm not the only one with rubbish parents right now. Why does he need to get rid of you?"

I instantly felt guilty for ranting about my dad. He'd worked so hard to keep things stable and happy for me since Mum was gone, and it wasn't like he could say, 'Actually, no, I don't want to do my job any more but could you keep paying me please while I just hang out on the beach with my daughter?'

"It's not really his fault. He's got to go on some research vessel out on the reef for, like, three weeks or something stupid. And I wasn't allowed to go with him."

"Did you tell him how annoyed you were?" Willa asked.

"Not ... exactly." By which I meant no, not at all. In fact, I'd actually told him it was totally fine and I completely understood.

Except it wasn't.

"Right," Willa said, with the sort of look that meant she didn't understand *me*. I was used to seeing that one. "So why the random woman? Was there literally no one else he could ask?"

"Usually, yes. But apparently everyone was away on holiday this time." We had a whole network of people who were happy to have me stay a night or two.

But this time he'd chosen *Mabel*.

Willa's eyes widened. She'd obviously been following the same train of thought as I had when Dad told me. "Oh! D'you reckon this woman's his new girlfriend?"

Bingo. And *that* was the number one reason I didn't

want to spend my summer with her.

"I know she is," I replied. "Because I asked him."

He'd looked embarrassed at the question and started stuttering in a way that was nothing like my laid-back, articulate father.

Mabel and I … we're old friends. And now we're seeing if maybe, well, we think we might, actually, um, be something more.

So she's your girlfriend? I'd asked. It had to have been going on for a while, yet I'd heard absolutely no mention of her until now.

That was the part that hurt.

I didn't want to tell you until we were sure it was going somewhere. We'd planned to talk to you after the Australia trip, he'd said sheepishly. *Introduce you properly, let you spend time together before… Well, anyway.*

He'd cut himself off, but I knew what that 'before' had meant. It meant 'before we get married'. Because I knew my dad better than anyone now Mum was gone. He'd been making noises about me needing more 'womanly influences' (as he put it) for months now. (Mostly I thought he was just terrified of having to give me the Talk on his own. You know, about periods and boys and stuff. Except Mum had already done that, before she died.)

Anyway. If he was sending me to stay with Mabel, she wasn't just a girlfriend. She was a prospective new mother.

And I *really* didn't need one of those, whatever Dad thought.

"Wow." Willa studied me, and somehow I was sure she read every one of my concerns in my face. And even weirder, it felt like she *understood*. "I'm guessing you're not keen on getting a new step-mum, huh? I know I wouldn't be."

"What's so bad about the random Italian aunt then?" I said, changing the subject.

Wriggling a little in her seat, Willa rolled her eyes dramatically, then leaned forwards. "Trust me. If you want *my* sob story, we need pastries first. Come on."

WILLA

I've been in enough airport lounges around the world to know that, whatever the time of day or night, there are *always* pastries.

Mandy, supposedly in charge of us, was clearly having some sort of life crisis given the way she was frowning at her phone and texting furiously. She barely looked up as Alice and I made our way through the connecting door to the *real* lounge and the pastries.

"Back in a minute," I called over my shoulder to pre-empt any questioning, but I doubted she was even listening. Her eyes were a little red round the rims, and she was reaching for the cookies.

I had considered making a run for it to avoid the Italian Summer Nightmare (as I was calling it) but the thing about airports was, unless you were getting on a plane, there weren't a lot of places to go. Even Mandy would probably raise the alarm if I disappeared completely, which would scupper my chances of finding another flight out of here, even if

I *could* manage to book a ticket with my mum's credit card.

The pastry table was at the far end of the business-class lounge, so Alice and I wandered past lots of people in suits and a few families with little kids to get at our snacks.

"I reckon her boyfriend just dumped her by text," I said.

Alice blinked a couple of times, clearly trying to piece together what I was talking about. "The UM woman? I just figured she was playing some game on her phone, or something. Do you think she's OK?"

I rolled my eyes. Clearly my new friend wasn't exactly a student of human nature.

My mum is always talking about a person's 'motivation' – what makes them do what they do. Usually she's referring to a character she's playing but it applies to real life too. People do things for a reason. I like trying to figure out what those reasons are.

Take Alice. She was obviously sulking because her dad had a new girlfriend – which was fair enough, I felt kind of the same about *my* dad too. But there was something else I hadn't figured out yet. Like, where was her mum? Abandoned her as a baby? Ran off with her piano teacher? Kidnapped by aliens? I'd get an answer by the time we landed in London.

"I'm sure she'll be fine. Come on."

After carrying our piled-high plates of *pain au chocolat* and maple pecan pastries back out of the business-class lounge, Alice and I settled into our seats in the Unaccompanied Minors room. Mandy looked up from her phone just long enough for me to see that her eyes were still red and sad.

"So," Alice said, nibbling on a *pain au chocolat*. "Now that we have pastries, what's this sob story of yours?"

I'd rehearsed my tale of woe repeatedly in the days leading up to this, in the mirror mostly, so I was well prepared for the question.

"My parents are Sarra and Scott Andrews," I said, and waited for the amazed look of recognition from Alice.

It didn't come.

"They starred together in *Heatherside*," I nudged, naming their most famous series. "For years, until they killed off Mum's character."

"The soap?" Alice asked, then shook her head. "I don't watch it, sorry."

"Mum's been in all sorts of shows and films since then, too many to name," I went on. But if she didn't watch *Heatherside* (*everyone* watches *Heatherside*, right?) Alice probably hadn't seen them either.

24

"So they're both actors," Alice said. I was starting to think she might be a bit slow on the uptake.

"Yes, Alice. They're actors. My dad's been on a kind of sabbatical from *Heatherside* for the last month or so," for reasons I really didn't want to go into, that were mostly waiting for the scandal to die down, "and now he's up in Edinburgh for the festival. You know, the Fringe?"

"I've heard of the Edinburgh Festival," Alice said, as if I should have known that. From the girl who didn't watch *Heatherside*.

"Anyway, I was supposed to be spending the next few weeks with him in London, but now he's in Edinburgh instead, performing in some weird comedy thing."

"What do you normally do during the holidays, then? If your parents are working?"

"*Usually* my dad's at home in Cheshire, filming for *Heatherside*, so it's not a problem." Or at least, it hadn't been, until he decided to run off with his much younger co-star, like the ultimate actor cliché. "But this year it all got complicated."

"So what happened?" Alice scooted closer on her chair. Obviously my life was fascinating to her. Naturally.

"Well, the plan was originally that Dad would be in London for the summer, so I'd stay with him. I was all signed up for this course at the theatre around the corner from his flat too."

I felt a pang again at missing the course – I'd worked so hard to convince Mum to let me go. She had claimed I wasn't old enough to think about an acting career yet, but what did she know?

There was another reason I wanted to do the course – one I hadn't told anybody. Rumour on the course message group was that the agent coming to the showcase would be the new casting director for *Heatherside*! Apparently they were adding a new family to the soap and needed two teenage daughters. If I got the part I'd be working with my dad every single day. Then there'd be no chance of him forgetting I existed, like he seemed to have done since he left.

"What changed?" Alice asked.

"The show Dad was in down in London got moved up to Edinburgh, and Mum's guest spot in the series here in LA turned into something more permanent and her filming schedule is crazy. She told Dad it was his turn to figure something out, since I was supposed to be with him anyway. I think she was hoping he'd take me to Edinburgh with him, but instead I'm—"

"Off to Italy and the random aunt," Alice finished my sentence. Then she frowned.

Part of me wondered whether it was just the filming schedule Mum was worried about, or if Veronica the Evil Agent had said something to her about me getting in the way. She couldn't go to all the showbiz parties with me there, and Veronica was always going on about networking.

As for Dad ... he didn't want me with him. He hadn't even *talked* to me about my ideas for how we could make it work if I went to Edinburgh with him, just packed me off to his half-sister in Italy, like an unwanted Christmas present.

The worst part was that, however mad I was at him, I still missed him. And the idea that I might be losing him for good ... terrified me.

Not that I was admitting it to Alice.

I shrugged. "Anyway I'm off to the aunt and you're off to London, and we can both be miserable about it together, all the way across the Atlantic."

"Which sucks," Alice said.

"It super does," I agreed.

"Maybe we should just swap summers," Alice said, laughing. "That way you'd get to go to your theatre course, and I'd get to avoid Mabel. Plus, I love

Italy and you hate it. If Mandy's anything to go by, I doubt the airline would notice." She nodded to where Mandy was now openly sniffling as she typed into her phone.

"They wouldn't," I agreed. "So what, we'd just swap suitcases and passports and pretend to be each other?" My mind was whirring with possibilities.

Alice laughed again. "Willa, it was a joke!"

"I know," I said.

But this was better than a joke. It was an opportunity. And we had a whole plane journey to figure it out.

ALICE

"Welcome aboard!" Mandy had handed us over to another flight attendant at the gate. Oonagh showed Willa, the two boys and me on to the plane, smiling broadly the whole time.

"How cute," she went on, as we filed past her. "Two brothers and two sisters. What a treat for me to look after you today!"

"We're not sisters," Willa and I said, in unison.

"Really?" Oonagh asked, as if we wouldn't know.

Willa rolled her eyes for the fifteenth time since I'd met her (I was counting), grabbed my arm, and pulled me over to our seats.

"We should really do it," she whispered, as Oonagh focused on getting the boys strapped in across the aisle. We were first on the plane, right at the front of the economy section, where the staff could keep their eyes on us.

"You're not serious," I replied.

"I am! We should totally swap places for the summer."

The excitement in Willa's eyes made me nervous. It was the same sort of gleam I saw in Dad's when he was all worked up about some research trip to a ridiculous place in the middle of nowhere with a reputation for murderous sea creatures or natural disasters.

She'd been pestering me about swapping summers the whole time in the queue for boarding at the gate, not to mention the walk from the UM lounge with Sad Mandy, but I'd mostly been tuning her out. I figured Willa was just being overdramatic about having to go to Italy when she was talking about 'reclaiming her life from her parents, the tyrants'.

Apparently not.

"You realize that's … kind of insane." Who pretended to be someone else for a whole summer? I mean, yes, the idea of spending my summer holiday in Italy was kind of wonderful, but also totally impossible. Right?

"It was your idea," Willa pointed out.

"Yeah, but I was joking." I *had* been joking. It was a joke. Just a joke.

"Yeah, but I'm not."

She stared me in the eyes as, behind her, the other passengers started to file on to the plane. Most of them looked tired or bored or resigned. None of them looked like they were contemplating the crazy.

But Willa was.

And against all my better judgement, so was I.

It was absolutely impossible, I knew that. But that didn't stop me imagining it. Italy, Mum's bucket list…

This was ridiculous.

"You can't really think we could actually do it. We'd get caught." Wouldn't we? I mean, there were passport controls and stuff for a reason.

"I bet you we wouldn't." Willa gave me a wicked grin as she fastened her seatbelt. "And we won't find out if we don't try."

"At which point we'll be in prison." I made myself think about *that*. How furious Dad would be with me.

Because otherwise, it was all too easy to imagine the benefits of being thousands of miles away from my prospective step-mum. I could just … avoid the situation entirely and hope it went away. Maybe Dad would lose interest in Mabel, once he got really stuck into the data from the research project. He was always hopping from one interest to another, after all. He hadn't even *mentioned* her until now, so how serious could he really be about her? Even the way he spoke about her: *an old friend ... maybe something more ... a possibility...* None of that sounded like true love to me.

If I just waited it out, maybe he'd realize that I didn't need another mother, and he wasn't all that interested in Mabel anyway.

What? It could happen. (In the back of my head I could hear my counsellor asking, 'Alice, do you ever feel that you try too hard to avoid difficult or upsetting situations?')

Well, if ever there was a situation worth avoiding, Mabel was it.

Willa waved a hand at me. "Prison?! We could totally talk our way out of it. Play it off as a mistake or a prank. It would be fine."

For the first time in my life, I was contemplating doing something outrageous. Something crazy. Dangerous, even.

This wasn't the sort of thing Alice Wright did. I studied hard, didn't worry my dad, smiled sadly when people told me how sorry they were about my mum, and didn't even let on to my closest friends how scared I was, all the time. Not that I could really say I had any close friends any more.

I'd tried to explain to Dad that I'd rather be alone

in Australia, waiting for him to come back, than on the other side of the Earth with some woman I'd never met before.

He said it wasn't safe. As if anything in this world is, really.

"Think about it," Willa said, her voice soft and persuasive. "I can spend the summer in London with your evil potential step-mother, and it doesn't even matter what she's like because I'll never have to see her again. In fact, I can put her off ever dating your dad again! You know, play the nightmare teen until she decides that dating a dad was the worst idea ever. It's the perfect solution to your problem!"

I had to admit, it was tempting.

If Mabel just *decided* she wasn't cut out for step-mothering and they broke up … that wouldn't be the worst thing in the world. And even though I'd only known Willa for an hour or two, I could already tell she'd be a much more difficult houseguest than I would.

"So what would *I* do while you were putting Mabel off step-mothering?" I couldn't believe I was even talking about this as a real plan. But I could already tell that Willa was going to keep on about it all the way to London if I didn't come up with some solid arguments as to why it wouldn't work. Something better than 'it's insane'. "Meet your aunt in Italy and pretend to be you? Won't she notice her niece has suddenly changed eye colour and dropped an inch or two around the…" I trailed off and waved my hand around my chest area.

Willa shrugged. "I've never met her, remember? She's meeting me at Heathrow to escort me, so getting you to Italy isn't a problem. And I doubt she's seen any recent photos of me. Mum said that Dad barely knows Aunt Sofia himself. They're half-siblings and they've never been close. Apparently Granddad Andrews ran off to Italy with a younger woman when Dad was a teenager, and Dad barely spoke to him ever again. I didn't even know he was in touch with Aunt Sofia."

I could imagine running off to Italy. I'd explore the beach, maybe find the nearest village and make friends with some local kids my age, learn Italian. Maybe I'd even get to have a summer crush…

"Apparently she fosters these other kids – there's one there about my age too. Built-in friends for the summer…" Willa said temptingly.

Of course, it couldn't be *that* tempting if *she* didn't want to spend time there, but I supposed she had her reasons. And it would be nice to have some company that wasn't Mabel…

"I bet Mabel has seen photos of me, though. Dad would have sent her some so she could recognize me at the airport, if nothing else. Your dad has probably done the same for your aunt."

There we go. A perfectly logical reason why the plan wouldn't work. I should be pleased.

But for some reason, I felt a little bit sad instead.

"That's true." Willa frowned. Then she lunged forwards and grabbed my phone from where it sat on my knee. "Right, show me the most recent photos of you he might have sent."

She held the phone as I unlocked it with my thumbprint, and scrolled through, trying to think which photos Dad might have picked.

"Um, this one, probably?" I angled the screen so she could see the shot of Dad and me at the Sydney Harbour Bridge, from the early, sightseeing part of our trip. "And maybe this one." A shot from last Christmas of me decorating the tree. He'd loved that photo so much he'd used it as his Christmas email card to his friends and colleagues, and printed it out for his desk. I squinted at it again, trying to see what he liked so much about it.

"Oh, that's a nice one." Willa pulled the phone closer for a better look. "You're smiling, for a start."

"I smile," I protested, but not very hard. I knew it was true that my resting face was sort of, well, thoughtful.

Willa flicked between the two photos, sending them to her own phone and studying them again.

"OK, well, this is easy. In the Sydney pic you're wearing jeans, T-shirt and that jacket open over it, right?" I nodded. It was what I nearly always wore. "Which is basically what you're wearing now. We'll switch clothes in the loo, so I look like you do in that photo. Neither shot is close up enough to see your eye colour, and if I part my hair like yours, we'll look enough alike for this to work. What about your passport photo?"

I pulled my passport from my bag and opened it at the right page. My own stony stare looked back at me. Willa glanced at it and laughed.

I shut it quickly, but she grabbed it from me. "Don't worry, mine is worse." She passed hers over and I took a peek. She was right. It *was* worse. "No one looks like their passport photo anyway," Willa went on. "We can just switch passports and no one will notice. This'll be easy."

Maybe she was right. I mean, those boys and the flight attendant had all thought we looked enough alike to be sisters. It *could* work.

Wait.

"I didn't say I would go along with this," I pointed out.

Willa flashed me a grin. "Yeah, but you're going to."

"How do you know?" I mean, *I* didn't.

"I have a sense about these things," Willa replied, sounding superior.

I flopped back into my seat, thinking hard, as the plane started to taxi along the runway.

"It'll never work. I mean, we'll get caught." It was inevitable.

"Not necessarily." Willa leaned over in front of me, straining her seatbelt. "When are you meeting your dad again?"

"Um, his flight gets into Heathrow in three weeks. The twenty-ninth. I was going to meet him at the airport, then we were going to get the train home to Cambridge together."

"Perfect! I'm supposed to fly back and meet my dad on the same day! It's clearly a sign."

"A sign of what?"

"That we're meant to do this!" Willa bounced a little in her seat. "Here's what we do. You fly back from Italy on the twenty-ninth, as me. I'll come to the airport and meet you and we can swap back before you meet your dad!"

"What about Mabel? She'll probably want to come meet Dad too."

"Not by the time I've finished with her," Willa said, with a sly grin. "Leave that part to me. I'll come up with something. Then I just have to hang out at the airport for a night then meet Dad. Mabel will dump your dad, my dad will go back to ignoring Aunt Sofia, and no one will ever know that we spent the summer in the wrong place."

Unless we told them. And I had to admit, it would make a great story. No one could ever call me boring again if I did this. I might not throw myself off boats into the ocean like my dad, or get invited to parties with the Year Elevens, like my ex-best friend Claire. But I could have my own adventure.

There were still a lot of details to work out. We needed to come up with plans for every possible eventuality, think of all the things that could happen to trip us up and get us caught – and I sensed that the planning part of this would fall on me. And even with the perfect plan there were still a *lot* of things that could go wrong.

In fact, I was almost certain that by the time I'd thought of them all, there was no way either one of us would want to go through with the swap.

But despite all my doubts and worries, there was one familiar phrase going round and round in my head.

"Death or glory, think of the story," I murmured. It was something my dad used to say, before he ran off on his latest trip around the globe. He stopped saying it after Mum died.

"What does that mean?" Willa asked.

I sat up straighter. "It means we need a plan."

WILLA

Death or glory. I liked the sound of that. Either we'd get caught at the first passport control or we'd get away with it and…

Well. That *would* be awesome. And not just because I'd get to spend summer in London and go to my theatre course.

I could almost imagine my parents' faces when they realized what I'd done.

Because, yeah, OK, I'd told Alice that no one would ever know. But that was just to get her to go along with my plans. What was the point of pulling a prank like this if no one realized they'd been pranked?

I would tell *everyone* about this. My friends, the people I met on set, maybe even the papers if Mum and Dad carried on being so awful. My parents were going to go absolutely nuts.

But by then I'd have spent the summer in London and I'd have a role on *Heatherside*. This summer could change *everything*. No way my parents could just ignore me and push me around after all that.

"So … how is this going to work? Hypothetically, I mean," Alice added quickly.

Above us, the 'Fasten seatbelt' sign pinged off. Normally, I'd be settling in with some snacks and a rubbish movie around now. But we had less than ten hours before we landed in London, and Alice was right – we needed to come up with a plan.

We were doing this.

Unclipping my seatbelt, I swivelled in my seat to face Alice, folding my leg up under me.

"OK, so here's what we do," I said, keeping my voice low. "Halfway through the flight, when they turn the lights out, we'll nip to the toilet and switch clothes. Then, when we come back, we'll sit in each other's seats, and swap all our stuff."

"Everything except phones," Alice said quickly. "We'd need our own phones, if we were going to do this. My dad will be out of range for video calls on the boat, but he'll still want to call me when he can."

"Yeah, that's a good idea." Apparently Alice was already three steps ahead of me – even if she was still pretending she might say no. I could tell she was as hooked on the idea as I was. "What about money? I've got a stash of euros you can have, plus I guess my dad has sorted things with my aunt. Oh, and there's my mum's credit card I can use. It's supposed to be for emergencies, but I reckon this counts. She's bound to have lifted the block now I'm out in the world without her, and I need to do some more revenge shopping."

Alice frowned. "Won't she get a bit suspicious if her credit card statement starts showing transactions from London?"

She had a point. Unfortunately.

I smiled as another thought occurred to me. "Then you'll have to do it!" I tugged my purse from my bag and showed Alice the credit card. "There's a piece of paper with the PIN on it somewhere too… Here. Promise me, if you go near *any* good shops, you'll buy clothes on this."

"O-kay," Alice said, drawing the word out as she shoved the credit card back in the purse.

She totally wasn't going to do it. Oh well. Aunt Sofia's farm was in the middle of nowhere anyway, so it wasn't like she'd have that many opportunities.

And if she did… Well, I had another three weeks to talk her into revenge spending on my behalf.

Alice carried on planning. "Dad said he'd transferred money to Mabel for anything I need this summer, as well as an allowance, so you should be covered there. Plus my mum always insisted on keeping an emergency twenty-pound-note somewhere, especially when travelling, so you'll have that if you need it. It's in the back of my passport case." Reaching into her bag, Alice pulled out a notebook and Biro, and began chewing on the end of the pen as she flipped through to find an empty page. "OK. We'll need to know as much as we can about each other. And you'll need to lose that American twang in your voice."

"I pick up accents easily," I said in broad American. Then I switched to my usual English accent. "I can drop it no problem."

"Good."

Alice smoothed out her notebook. I twisted my head to try to read the page that had writing on, but she covered it with her arm before I could get a good look. I glanced away and pretended I hadn't been interested anyway.

What mattered was that she was talking about our plan like it was happening, at last.

"We could email each other a sort of profile," I suggested, as she tapped her pen against the empty page. "Everything You Need To Know About Me, you know? Enough that we can fake it, anyway."

"That's a good idea," Alice said.

I shrugged. "My mum took over from another actor

on a show once, playing the same part and hoping the viewers didn't notice she looked totally different. When she got the role, the director sent over like a character bible, telling her everything she needed to know to play the part. I figured this is kind of the same."

"I guess it is." Alice smiled. "You said you were supposed to be going to a course at a theatre in London. Do you want to be an actor like your parents, then?"

"Maybe." As in, 'definitely, absolutely, try to stop me' maybe. I'd grown up in TV studios, on film sets, backstage at theatres. I'd watched my parents and their colleagues be hundreds and hundreds of different people, doing different jobs, loving different people, experiencing different lives. The idea of getting an ordinary office job was just … boring. What other job in the world let you try on a different life with every part you played?

And playing Alice for the summer would be my first starring role.

"What about you?" I asked in return. "Do you want to be a professor like your dad?"

Alice lifted one shoulder in a half-shrug. "I don't really know *what* I want to be, to be honest. Maybe something with languages? I like French and Spanish at school. I wish we'd studied Italian…"

Suddenly Oonagh appeared at our seats. "Now, how are my two girls doing? Are you settled in all right? You don't need anything?"

Before we could answer, some guy started calling for her in an annoyed tone.

"So you're fine? Great!" With another smile, she dashed off to deal with the man who was still yelling.

"Yeah, I don't think we need to worry about her noticing we've switched stuff," Alice said quietly, as we watched her bustle away down the aisle. "She's barely had time to look at us since we got on the plane."

"So all we need to do is learn enough about each other to pass until we can email full details, yeah?"

Alice nodded. "I guess so. I mean, if we were really doing this."

I gave her a look. "Alice. We're doing this. Right?"

She chewed her lip, still looking uncertain. But I could see in her eyes that she wanted to as much as I did.

"I mean, how bad could it be if things go wrong?" I pressed.

"We could get arrested and thrown in jail and ruin our futures."

She was such a pessimist. "The worst that will happen is we get yelled at, and I'll tell them I forced you to go along with it or something. OK?"

"You'd take the blame?"

I shrugged. "At least if I got arrested my parents would have to pay me *some* attention, right?"

That made her smile, just a little.

"So, where were we?" I said.

"Um, we were talking about what we needed to know about each other until we can get full dossiers written and sent," Alice said.

I rolled my eyes at the word 'dossiers'. Only Alice would call it something so dorky.

"Well, what do we *already* know?"

Alice looked down at her blank notebook page as if it would help, then up at me again. "OK, well, all I know so far is that your name is Willa Andrews, your parents are actors and you want to be one too, and you're going to stay with your Aunt Sofia somewhere in Italy."

"I think it's near Naples, if that helps?" I screwed up my face trying to remember what else Mum had told me. "I can't remember anything else about it."

"I guess if you don't know where it is it doesn't matter that I don't either."

"Good point."

"So, what else do I need to know?" she asked, and

I realized what a weird question it was to answer.

What do I need to know to pretend to be you?

Alice would have my clothes, my passport, my identification. She'd have my aunt there, already believing she was me.

What else was I, apart from my belongings and my family?

"Um ... I'm fourteen years old," I started.

"Same as me," Alice put in.

"Great, that'll make things easier to remember. So you've just finished Year Nine, right? Like me?" Alice nodded, so I carried on. "I grew up in Cheshire with Mum and Dad, and I go to Croftdean School there. My best friends are – well, were – Noemi and Tara, plus there was a whole gang of others, but they don't really matter—"

"Wait. Were?" Alice asked. "What happened?"

I sighed. I guessed it was stupid to think that Alice could pretend to be me without knowing the whole awful story about my parents' break-up.

"It turned out my friends were more interested in the fact that my parents were famous than in me as a person," I explained. "When my dad left *Heatherside* on sabbatical this spring, he left my mum too. Like, permanently. Ran off with the actress who played his teenage daughter on the show when she got written out. I mean, she's twenty-seven in real life, but still, it's pretty gross." And it didn't feel great, either, being left behind. "Anyway, at that point my friends decided it was far more fun talking *about* me behind my back than *to* me."

Alice winced. "Not cool. I'm sorry."

"Yeah. I guess that's why my mum is so determined to make it in LA right now. To show she doesn't need him. Prove that she can be a bigger star without him anyway."

I pulled up a photo of me and Mum together to show Alice.

"She's pretty," Alice said, as she stared at the photo of Mum and me in matching ripped jeans and leather jackets. Mum had posted the photo on Twitter after the break-up with the caption 'Andrews girls hit LA'.

I wondered what she'd post now I'd gone. Agent Veronica would probably have some ideas. At least I'd got to take the jacket with me. I reckoned it would be just right for London in the summer.

Except it wouldn't be in London with me, I realized. Alice would have it, along with the rest of the contents of my suitcase. And I'd have Alice's battered khaki canvas jacket instead.

Maybe I hadn't thought this plan all the way through, I realized, looking down at Alice's coat, jeans and T-shirt. Never mind missing my family – I would *definitely* miss my wardrobe. There was the most incredible Forever 21 red top I'd bought on Mum's card sitting in my suitcase that I hadn't even got to wear yet...

But looking at that photo, remembering that day with Mum, reminded me that there was something very important I needed to know about Alice before we swapped lives.

"Alice... What's the deal with your mum?"

She looked away, but I could see she'd gone pale.

"Mum ... she died. About four years ago now."

I bit my lip. No wonder Alice didn't want some other woman coming in and taking her mum's place. It was bad enough my dad running off with another woman, but at least I still had them both.

"I'm sorry." That was what you said when someone told you something awful and sad, right? Mum was better at it than me. I'd watched her, taking someone's hand, making sympathetic noises, saying all the right things. But I just felt awkward and wrong.

Alice shook her head and sent me a slightly wobbly smile. "You needed to know anyway, before you meet

49

Mabel. Now, send me that photo of you and your mum."

"Why?" I frowned, but did as she asked.

Alice didn't answer. Instead, a few swipes later, she held up her phone to show me the home screen, featuring me and Mum.

"No one would think this wasn't your phone now, right?" She peered at the photo again. "And I guess it could just about pass as me, as long as I'm wearing your clothes…"

I looked at Alice, and at the photo again. "Maybe I can do something with your hair," I suggested.

She looked relieved. "That would help." She picked up a strand of her long, dark hair. "I never know what to do with it."

"Online tutorials," I told her. "I'll send you some links. And in the meantime, tell me all about you. Or, rather, me, for the next few weeks."

It was time to get into character.

ALICE

The midnight clothes swap went without a hitch, even though I spent the whole time I was changing into Willa's clothes reminding myself that this was crazy.

We switched passports and hand luggage too. I held on to my phone and my laptop, but otherwise all my worldly possessions were suddenly Willa's.

And I had hers.

There were no books in Willa's carry-on bag, I realized quickly, although there were a few magazines and the headphones she'd been using with her tablet. I pulled those out and she held out her hand to take them. Using my cheap ear buds instead was a step too far for Willa.

I smothered a giggle at the thought. Willa would be wearing my clothes, my underwear, living my life for the next three weeks – but somehow *ear buds* were the line we were drawing?

Willa just shrugged when I mentioned it. "You can have many things, but not my Beats headphones."

It was fair enough. Willa's over-ear, wireless headphones probably cost more than the entire contents of my rucksack.

"Anything else you want from in here?" I asked in a whisper. I pulled out a make-up bag, and opened the zip. It was filled with the sort of expensive make-up I only ever saw on TV adverts. I wasn't sure what Willa was going to make of my lip-gloss, powder and mascara-for-special-occasions make-up bag.

Willa reached out for the brow kit at the top of the bag, then pulled her hand back and shook her head. "What about you? Anything you want to keep from your bag?"

I bit my lip and, after a moment's thought, reached out to retrieve my notebook and small pencil case. I might be *pretending* to be Willa, but I was still Alice really, and I got ... unsettled if I didn't have somewhere to write down all my thoughts and feelings.

The counsellor I saw after Mum died had suggested the journaling, and three years later it was such a part of me I couldn't imagine not doing it. I'd just have to be super careful that no one found it while I was in Italy. And maybe write in code or something. Or maybe just English would do, actually, since I was in a foreign country.

A horrible thought occurred to me. "Your aunt *does* speak English, right?" How had I not thought of that before?

Willa shrugged, as if to say 'not my problem'. "I guess so. I don't speak Italian, so she won't be expecting you to."

That wasn't quite the same thing. Oh well. I supposed I'd muddle through. Being immersed in a language was the best way to learn it, anyway. I had a knack for languages, my teachers said.

"OK, time to fix your hair," Willa said, and I tried not to groan.

I'd spent years battling to make my hair do *anything* besides hang limply on either side of my head. Usually these days I just parted it on the right and hoped for the best.

Apparently that wasn't enough for Willa. Her hair was parted on the other side, with a sort of zigzag part, falling in loose waves over her shoulders. I was pretty sure mine would never look like that.

"It doesn't need to," Willa said, when I expressed my concern. "Look, I'll put it in a simple braid for you now, OK? Then you can watch some tutorials on your laptop when you get there for some more ideas."

"You realize your aunt probably doesn't know or

care how you wear your hair?" I pointed out, as she tugged the front of my hair into three sections and started braiding, taking in extra hair from the sides on each turn, as she weaved it round the front of my head, down behind my left ear. "I mean, it's long and dark like yours. That's probably enough, right?"

"Who said I was doing this for my aunt?" Willa asked, as she tied off my braid below my left shoulder, then fiddled with the higher-up bits, tugging on parts of the plait to make it looser. "I just think it'll look pretty this way. See?"

She pulled a mirror out of her – my – bag, and held it up for me to examine the results. The plait looked like the sort of complicated style that took hours to create but Willa had managed it in no time and I had to admit, it *did* look pretty. I was certain I'd never be able to recreate it on my own, though.

"It's a Dutch braid," Willa explained. "Looks more complicated than it is."

"I love it." My hair had never looked so good. I looked like a different person.

I looked like Willa.

And suddenly I started to believe that maybe I could do this.

Three hours later – 1 a.m. LA time, and 9 a.m.

London – we landed at Heathrow, both of us exhausted from the lack of sleep but totally wired. Oonagh passed us over to yet another Unaccompanied Minors person, who ticked us off on his list as we introduced ourselves as each other. Willa's name felt weird in my mouth, but Willa seemed to have no problem at all saying, "I'm Alice Wright."

Then it was time to go through passport control.

My chest tightened as we joined a short queue, and the red leather jacket felt unfamiliar and too heavy on my shoulders. As I clutched Willa's passport I realized my palm was slippery with sweat. This was our first real test.

What's the worst thing that could happen? My mum's voice sounded in my head, the words she would always say when I was worried about something – school or friends or a choir concert or whatever.

The worst thing that could happen this time was that we'd get caught out. We'd claim that we'd mixed up our passports by mistake (Willa had already thought of that on the plane) and switch back. Even if they didn't believe us, we could probably pass it off as a prank on the UM person, like Willa had suggested. One way or another, I'd spend the summer in London after all.

Now, what's the best thing that could happen?

Mum always wanted us to look for the good in the world. The excitement, the magic. The best things.

The best thing that could happen was… I'd spend an amazing summer in Italy. I'd make new friends, learn a new language, see new places … visit that waterfall. Then hopefully by the time I headed back to the UK to meet Dad, Mabel would be a thing of the past.

Besides, it was too late to turn back now. Forcing myself to smile, I handed over Willa's passport and waited as the official scrutinized it.

Was he taking too long? It felt like he was taking too long. I bit the inside of my cheek to keep the truth from jumping out of my mouth.

"Welcome back to the UK, Miss Andrews," he said, handing me back the passport.

I tried to take it without grabbing, then looked back as Willa collected my passport from the official at the next desk over. She looked strangely more like me with her hair parted differently. Then she threw me a grin that was pure Willa.

We'd done it. Part one complete.

Now we needed to convince Aunt Sofia and Mabel.

"What does your suitcase look like?" Willa

whispered in my ear as we approached the luggage carousel.

"Navy blue with a light blue ribbon on the handle. Yours?"

"Pink and lime green flowers."

"Of course."

It took real effort not to grab my navy suitcase when I saw it come down the conveyor belt. Instead, I nudged Willa. And when, a few minutes later, I saw a neon pink flowery case appear, I didn't need her to tell me.

"Right, shall we go find your relatives?" the UM guy asked us all.

"Mabel's not my relative," Willa said, as me. "She's my dad's girlfriend." Her tone made it very clear what she – or I – felt about that.

Maybe it was for the best that we'd be in different countries. It was already getting confusing!

The arrivals hall was packed with people meeting their loved ones, and drivers holding up signs. Our UM guide led us to a small 'Information' stand. Willa and I hung back as he prepared to address the people milling around it.

Suddenly, I felt the panic rising inside me again as I realized that this was it. I was Willa now. My breathing got faster, and I couldn't slow it down, and I clenched my fists tight – until the real Willa grabbed my hand.

"Death or glory, right?" she whispered.

"Think of the story," I finished softly, letting out a longer breath at last. "You'll message me as soon as you can?"

"Before you even make it to Italy," Willa promised. "Good luck being me!"

"You too."

And then the UM guy was talking again, and there was no time to say anything more.

"Right, can I ask that you all have your paperwork and ID ready as you come forwards to collect your Unaccompanied Minors?" he said, and there was a rustle of paper from the group.

"Willa Andrews," he said, and Willa gave me a small push forwards, as a youngish woman with dark hair and dark eyes approached the stand.

"Hi, I'm Sofia Toscana, here to collect my niece Willa." She handed over a form and an Italian passport and waited for the guy to check it.

I glanced back at Willa, who gave me a quick thumbs up before ducking behind some other passengers.

"OK." The man handed back the passport and

paperwork and gave Sofia a nod.

I was up.

"Hi, Aunt Sofia," I said, a little nervously. I was glad Willa was hiding. Otherwise the similarity between her and her aunt might be too obvious to ignore. Half-aunt or not, she had Willa's eyes, and the same hair too.

"Willa!" Sofia burst into a broad, unsuspecting grin, and wrapped me up tight in her arms. "It's so wonderful to meet you! I couldn't believe it when your dad said you were fourteen already. You grew up!"

I gave a cautious smile. "Well, that happens, I guess."

"And you look so like the photos I've seen of your mother!" She took my suitcase handle from me, and started wheeling it across the arrivals hall. I risked a glance back at Willa, and saw her standing stiff-backed as she was hugged by a tall blond woman.

Mabel.

I looked away again quickly before she spotted me watching, my heart racing.

"Antonio has our bags over at the restaurant. We've a while before our flight home, so we thought we'd take you to brunch!"

"Great!" I said, trying desperately to remember if Willa had ever mentioned an Antonio. "Um, is Antonio one of your foster children?" I guessed. "Wi— I mean, Dad mentioned that you had some other kids staying with you."

"That's right! Antonio's the eldest – you'll meet his brother and sister when we get home. We were over here looking at UCL for Antonio for next year. He's half English, you see, like me, and he wanted to consider a UK university. Look, there he is!" Sofia waved towards a chain restaurant ahead of us, and a tall, dark, utterly gorgeous guy a few years older than me stood up and waved back.

Yeah, I was almost certain Willa hadn't known about Antonio. Apparently when her dad mentioned the foster kids, he hadn't told her that one of them was seventeen and gorgeous. No way Willa would have given up the chance to stay in Italy with him! Maybe my hopes of ticking 'first crush' off my Life To-Do List weren't so crazy after all.

I checked behind me one last time, but Willa and Mabel were already gone.

My braid swished over my shoulder, and I tried on a Willa smile. Somehow, I felt like I really was a different person already.

Maybe not being Alice for a while would be good for me. A chance to try on a new personality. A more confident and spontaneous one.

A happier one, even.

WILLA

"Alice Wright?"

As the man behind the desk called Alice's name, I stopped watching her walk away with my aunt and tried to give my full attention to the role at hand. Even if a part of me was still thinking how like Dad Aunt Sofia looked. Just younger and lots prettier.

Tucking my hair behind my ears like I'd watched Alice do every time she got nervous about our plan, I stepped forwards. I tried for Alice's tentative smile, and hoped that her new step-mum-to-be wouldn't notice the lack of freckles across my nose, or the darkness of my eyes.

A blond woman, taller than me, with her hair in choppy waves to her shoulders, jerked forwards to give me an awkward hug.

"Alice! It's so great to meet you at last. Your dad has told me so much about you. I'm Mabel. Which you probably already guessed." Her hug got even more awkward when I didn't hug her back – but that was part of my role too, right? Hating my prospective Evil Step-mother.

"Um, I thought we could take the Tube to my flat?" Mabel stepped back, her eyes darting from my face to my suitcase to over my shoulder where I'd seen the sign for the Underground. She flicked her hair nervously away from her face. Huh. Maybe she and Alice would have had more in common than Alice had thought. "Unless you want to eat here first? Are you hungry? Or do you just want to get home for a nap? To help with the jet lag? I mean, either's fine by me. Whatever you want."

She even rambled like Alice. "Tube is fine," I said, hoisting Alice's rucksack on to my shoulder. It was a sensible, dark blue waterproof one, with tiny daisies on it. Very Alice. God only knew what she had in it, but it weighed a ton. I guessed I'd find out when I unpacked. Alice had checked every inch of my bag on the plane, but I'd only had a quick peek at hers. I hadn't *seen* any hand weights, but maybe I'd missed them…

Mabel took my suitcase for me, and we walked side by side towards the escalator down to the Underground. When I was travelling with my parents, we would get a cab to Euston station for our train home. It was kind of fun to be taking the Tube like a real Londoner.

I wondered where Mabel lived. Was it anywhere near Oxford Street and all the good shops? Because I *really* needed to do something about Alice's clothes, if the ones I was wearing were representative of what was in her suitcase. There hadn't been time to switch anything from our main cases, which meant I only had Alice's bras for the next three weeks, other than the one I was wearing. Too-small bras were *not* a good look, never mind the fashion don'ts I was sure the rest of her wardrobe held. Alice's clothes suited Alice fine, I was sure. They just weren't very *me*.

Even if I was being Alice, that didn't mean I couldn't upgrade her fashion sense, just a little bit.

"My flat's up in North London," Mabel said, as she bumped my – or Alice's – case down a few steps. "But we can get the Tube pretty much straight from here, as long as you don't mind a little bit of a walk at the other end."

"I've been basically sitting down for ten hours," I pointed out. "A walk is fine."

"Great!" Mabel seemed overly pleased at my response.

We negotiated the ticket barriers and the escalators

easily enough. Mabel had already bought me an Oyster card and loaded it with credit. She'd put it in a cute card-holder with seashells on it.

"Your dad told me you loved the seaside," she said, as she handed it to me.

"Right. Yeah." Beaches were fine for sunbathing and stuff but I preferred cities. But Alice had said her dad was a marine biologist, I suddenly remembered. "Love the sea. Just like Dad."

Mabel's nervous expression transformed to a warm smile. "He's definitely a water person, isn't he?"

Oh God. She wanted to talk about her *boyfriend* with me.

As the Tube train rattled to a stop at the platform, I realized I was going to have to take control of the dialogue.

"Tell me about your flat," I said quickly, as we took our seats. "Is it nice?"

"I like it," Mabel said, in the sort of way that told me I probably shouldn't be expecting too much. Certainly not the four- and five-star hotel standard I'd got used to. "It's not huge, but it's got two bedrooms, so you'll have your own room. And it's above a florist's shop, which I love. It means that the scent of the flowers wafts up in the mornings and makes everything smell sweet." Her eyes widened suddenly. "Wait. You don't have hay fever, do you? I don't think your dad said…"

Did Alice have hay fever? I had no idea. Maybe that was something we should cover in our profiles – allergies and medical issues. Along with, you know, everything else. But since I was the one who'd be living on top of a flower shop, it was just as well that I didn't suffer from seasonal allergies.

"No hay fever," I assured her, and Mabel relaxed.

"Oh good." I wondered what she'd have done if I had. Moved house, maybe. She seemed so determined to make this visit perfect, I almost felt sorry for her. However hard she tried to impress me, it wouldn't make any difference to her relationship with Alice's dad, or Alice.

Mabel reached into her handbag and pulled out a thick file full of leaflets and printouts. "Now, I didn't know what you had planned for these next few weeks, or what you've already seen or done before in London, so I just brought everything." She dumped the file on my lap with a wide smile. "Your dad told me that you like to plan ahead. And I know that coming to stay with me wasn't in the plan – for any of us, really. But I think it could be a great opportunity for us to get to know each other, and I want to make things as easy for you as I can. It's a long ride back to mine, so I thought we could get planning together on the way!"

I'd been awake for over twenty-four hours, travelling for about half of that, and I'd changed my whole identity somewhere in the middle. The last thing I wanted to do was plan out my whole holiday – especially since I was more of a make-it-up-as-I-go-along girl.

But Alice wasn't. And I was Alice now.

So I plastered on a smile and opened the folder. "Great."

Mabel beamed back at me.

My cheeks were starting to hurt. I tugged out a leaflet about Buckingham Palace to hide my face so I could stop smiling and start figuring out how I was going to put Mabel off step-mumming for good.

ALICE

From: **AliceJWright@mymail.co.uk**

To: **WillaMayAndrews@purpleworld.com**

Re: **Dossier**

Hi Willa

So, I guess you're in London now... Hope it's going OK with Mabel.

Here's all the information I could think of about me. Send me yours when you can? Your aunt is already asking stuff I don't know.

Alice x

ALICE JOSEPHINE WRIGHT

Age: 14, same as you. My birthday is June 9th.

Height: 158cm

Eye colour: Green

Of course, since you can't change your height or eye colour, there's probably not much point in telling you this stuff. So on to the more interesting stuff.

Family: I'm an only child. My dad's a Professor of Marine Biology at Anglia Ruskin University in Cambridge. My mum ... well, like I told you on the plane, she died a few years ago from breast cancer.

My Granny and Granddad Wright (Sheila and Dave) live up in Scotland, and my Grandpa John (Mum's dad) is in Spain. He moved there after Grandma Wendy died. I've got an Auntie Louise in Newcastle, but we don't see her much. And that's about it for family.

Friends: My best friend is called Claire, and we've known each other since Year Five. Actually, we haven't been that 'best' for the last term or two, since she started hanging out with the Year Tens and Elevens in her dance classes. But Dad doesn't know that (because he'd only worry) so it doesn't matter much. My other friends are mostly people I know from my swimming club, choir or Guides.

Interests & Hobbies: I like reading, TV, music, the usual stuff. I swim most weeks, go to Guides on a Thursday, and sing in the school choir and play flute in our school orchestra (I'm not very good though).

History: I was born in Southampton, and we lived in Bristol and North Wales before we moved to Cambridge when I was ten.

Medical Information: I'm allergic to strawberries, and I bet Dad has told Mabel that, so don't eat any when she can see you. Other than that, I'm pretty healthy.

Other Information: That's kind of it. Oh, except... I don't know how much Dad has told Mabel about me, or what she'll mention. So just in case... I saw a counsellor after Mum died, because I was having some issues with anxiety. She was great, and taught me some techniques for not stressing out about stuff. I think I might be using them all this summer! So, yeah. If Mabel mentions it, that's a thing. And if you need to know any of the techniques, just in case, I'll send them over.

Good luck!

Sofia chattered all the way through brunch, telling me about Antonio's university visit, about our travel plans from here, about how she missed everything back home – especially her husband Mattias, and Antonio's siblings, Luca and Rosa.

"We've only been gone two days, Sofia," Antonio said, in gorgeously accented English. He hadn't said much over brunch, but I figured that was because it was hard to get a word in edgeways when you were around Sofia. Or maybe he was just the strong and silent type… (Normally, Claire was the one who was obsessed with boys, and I was the sensible one. But then, Antonio wasn't like the normal boys in our school. He was almost a man – which was just one of many, many reasons I knew he'd never be interested in me. Even if I really *was* Willa. Who would totally be kicking herself for the swap when I told her about Antonio.)

"Really? It feels like longer." Sofia handed me the basket of croissants. "Have another one. It's a long journey home." I took one, thinking that, at this rate, I was going to name this 'the summer of pastries'.

Sofia was friendly and kind and lively – and she

never stopped talking. Which would have been fine, if she didn't also ask so many questions. Questions I had no answers to, because they were about people I'd never met, places I'd never been, or a life I'd never lived.

"I was reading about your mum's new show, Willa. It sounds so exciting! When do they finish filming, do you know?"

"Um … the end of the summer, I think." It was a total guess, but Sofia seemed satisfied.

"And your dad's show in Edinburgh sounds hilarious. I wish I'd had the chance to go over and see it, now we're back in touch after all these years, but, ah, well." She shrugged, and reached for another pastry. "Maybe next year. Will he go back again, do you think?"

"Perhaps?" I said uncertainly.

I *really* needed Willa to send me her dossier. The basic information we'd exchanged on the plane wasn't going to be nearly enough to get me through the rest of the summer if Sofia kept asking questions like this.

Fortunately, after brunch, Sofia was happy to read, and Antonio was watching some film on his tablet, as we sat at the gate waiting for our plane to Naples, so I managed to avoid having to answer too many questions by listening to music on my phone. Then, once the plane took off, I told them the long flight had caught up with me and closed my eyes, pretending to sleep. Apparently, at some point I stopped pretending, because the next thing I knew, Sofia was shaking me awake as we came in to land.

Antonio drove us from the airport to Sofia's house. "He needs the practice," Sofia had said, handing him the keys with a teasing smile. Given the way the car swerved around, he did.

The roads twisted out of the city and into the countryside. I drank in the view from the windows, forgetting for a while that I was Willa now, and just remembering all the wonderful times I'd had in Italy as Alice instead.

The air smelled different here. In Australia it had been sea salty and fresh. Back home in Cambridge, it just smelled like coffee and bikes and buses, and there was always the sound of buskers and a buzz of conversation.

Here in Italy, there was the same warm, slow feel to the air and the scent of leaves and sunshine that I remembered from before. I couldn't find all the words I needed to describe the emotions it brought up in me, but I knew it felt like coming back to where

I belonged. Where I'd last been truly happy, that summer before Mum died.

"Here we are," Sofia said softly, as we took one last bend, and her home came into view.

The farmhouse looked like a jigsaw that had been put together wrong, with chimneys and windows in all sorts of odd places. Extra bits had obviously been added on to the main building over the years, extending it out in all directions. It was a patchwork house, and I loved it on sight.

Antonio stopped the car in front of the house, just as three people came barrelling out through the front door.

The first was a girl, a few years younger than me, with huge blue eyes and sandy brown hair that came down almost to her waist. The second was a boy around my age, with darker, warier eyes, who looked a little bit like a younger, less gorgeous Antonio. The third was a big, Italian man, whose eyes and mouth crinkled up in a smile at the sight of Sofia. Rosa, Luca and Mattias, I guessed.

"You're home, *cara*." The man moved forwards with big strides and, as Sofia climbed out of the passenger seat, wrapped her up in his arms. "We missed you."

"Mattias doesn't cook half as well as you," the boy

told Sofia, but he was watching me. I realized they must be speaking English for my benefit, even if I hadn't been introduced yet.

Sofia turned in Mattias's arms to address me. "Willa, this is my husband, your Uncle Mattias. And these scamps are Antonio's brother and sister, Luca and Rosa."

"Pleased to meet you all," I said politely.

Rosa dashed forwards and threw her arms round my waist. "We can be friends?" she asked. "I'm eight. How old are you?"

"Fourteen," I told her. Rosa shot a glare back at the younger brother.

"That's the same as Luca. I think you're nicer, though."

I'd never had a brother or sister (neither had Willa) so I didn't have any experience of sibling rivalry. Still, I could imagine that being the youngest of three, with two older brothers, might not always be the most fun.

"I'll try to be," I promised.

Rosa beamed while, behind her, Luca rolled his eyes.

"Is it true that your mum and dad are movie stars?" Rosa asked, in a hushed, awed voice.

"Um, I guess… Well, TV stars… Um, they're both

actors, anyway." Why hadn't I asked Willa more questions about her parents' shows?

Luckily Rosa didn't seem to need details. "Wow!" She grinned. "That makes you a star too!"

I laughed. "It really doesn't." That much at least I was sure of.

"Now, did you put that lasagne in the oven?" Sofia gazed up at her husband – who was a good head and shoulders taller than her.

"Of course," Mattias replied. "And I was just making the salad to go with it."

"There was lasagne?" Luca asked. "Why couldn't we have had *that* for dinner yesterday?"

"Sofia's lasagne is the best," Rosa whispered to me.

"Because then there wouldn't have been a special dinner waiting for Willa when she arrived," Sofia said calmly. Then, disentangling herself from Mattias's hug, she clapped her hands together. "Now, inside, everyone. Antonio, Luca, can you bring the bags, please?"

"I can carry my own suitcase," I said, moving towards the car, but Antonio stopped me with a smile that made my stomach feel funny. Or maybe that was just the jet lag.

"You're the visitor. I'll do it."

Sofia linked her arm with mine, and led me into the house. "Tonight, you're our guest," she explained. "Tomorrow, you're family."

"And then you get *chores*," Luca added, as he wheeled Willa's glaringly bright suitcase past me, into the tiled hallway. Apparently his brother had passed on the job, despite his words.

"You can help me feed the chickens!" Rosa said, clapping her hands as she galloped past.

Sofia laughed. "They make it sound like a work camp! I promise, this will be a real holiday for you, Willa. But it's true, on a farm, there are always plenty of chores to go around."

"That's fine by me." It would be nice to feel part of something, to feel useful – rather than just sitting around waiting for Dad to come back and tell me about his day.

And besides, helping out around the place might make me feel a little less guilty about lying to everyone.

"Perfect! You know, Willa, I think we're all going to have a wonderful summer together." Sofia squeezed my arm, and the guilt rose up again. "Now let's show you to your room."

My room was at the far end of one of the add-on parts of the farmhouse, up a narrow, bare wood staircase. Luca rushed past us again on his way down as we started to climb – I presumed my case was up in my room already – and dashed off round a corner to who knew where. I had no idea how many rooms the house had, but I supposed Sofia needed them for the three kids – and any others she fostered.

"Have Antonio, Luca and Rosa been with you long?" I asked, as we climbed the stairs.

"Eighteen months only," Sofia replied. "And Antonio will be off again next year to university."

"Will Luca and Rosa stay?"

Sofia shrugged. "That depends. We will see." I wondered what had brought the three of them to Sofia's farm in the first place.

Maybe I'd find out, over the summer.

Reaching the top of the staircase, Sofia threw open a heavy wooden door, and suddenly we were bathed in warm light.

"Oh!" I swallowed hard as I looked around the huge room. The floorboards were bare but painted white to match the sheets on the old, iron-framed bed pushed against the wall. On the end of the bed was a patchwork quilt in faded shades of blue and green, and there was a white dressing table and stool against the other wall, with a large, oval mirror above it. Behind the door was a heavy, dark wood wardrobe twice the size of my tiny IKEA one at home. Willa's suitcase leaned against the wall beside it.

But the best thing of all was the large picture window with a bench running under it, covered with cushions. Thin, gauzy curtains fluttered in the breeze from the open window and I crossed the floor to look out over fields of olive trees, and all the way to the sea in the distance.

"Is it OK?" Sofia asked.

I turned to her and beamed. "It's absolutely perfect. Thank you."

Sofia answered my smile with one of her own. "Good. I want you to feel at home here this summer, Willa."

And despite the fact that the name she used wasn't mine, and that she wasn't really my aunt, I nodded. "I think I will."

Then Mattias called up the stairs to tell us dinner was ready, and my stomach rumbled in response.

Sofia laughed. "Come. Lasagne first, unpacking later."

WILLA

I kind of missed most of Mabel's apartment when we arrived. I mean, I know we climbed some metal steps at the back of the building, and crossed the roof of the florist shop below to get to the front door. But then she showed me up the stairs inside (is it still a flat if it has two floors? How does that even work?) to my room and I basically passed out on the bed.

When I woke up, it was already late afternoon. Rubbing my eyes, I sat up and took in my new home for the summer. The room was small, and the bed I'd crashed out on was a day bed, rather than a real one. A hanging rail had been shoved in the corner with some hangers on it, and Alice's suitcase sat beside it. There was a small chest of drawers, and a huge desk with row upon row of shelves full of books above it.

I guessed this was probably Mabel's study, when she didn't have a teenage houseguest. But for the next few weeks, it was all mine.

Unpacking could wait, I decided, so I headed down the stairs to find Mabel in the small, square kitchen, chopping salad vegetables.

"You're awake," she said with a smile. "I hope you don't mind, but I just picked up some stuff from the deli for dinner. I wasn't sure how hungry you'd be, what with the jet lag. It's a long way to travel, all the way from Australia, especially on your own."

I opened my mouth to tell her I'd only come from LA, then shut it again quickly. *Alice* had travelled from Australia.

"I don't think my body knows what day it is," I admitted. *Or* who *it is.* I took a seat at the bistro table. "But I could eat."

Dinner was delicious but awkward. Over lasagne and salad (seriously, I might as well have been in Italy) Mabel asked me endless questions that I had no idea of the answers to. By the time she brought out dessert (ice cream – great choice) I'd already fudged my way through conversations on:

Australia (never been, but my mum used to watch a lot of *Home and Away*, so I used that and hoped she'd never seen it, and that my claim to have spent all my time at the beach was believable);

My dad (squirmed awkwardly and hoped she'd assume it was because I was freaked out by the idea of her dating him);

School (basically just talked about my own school nightmares, only made them more boring, so they'd sound more believably 'Alice');

Books (smiled and nodded as if I knew what she was talking about).

Finally, dinner was over. I offered to help with the dishes (seemed Alice-y) but Mabel waved me away to the lounge while she loaded the dishwasher.

Covering my mouth with my hand to hide my yawn, I made my way through to the lounge, which was set up with two armchairs rather than a big sofa like we had a home. (In fairness, there wouldn't have been space for our sofa. Mabel's lounge was ... cosy, let's say.) I picked a chair and curled up in it.

This was weird. Being in someone else's house, someone I'd never met, someone who didn't even know my real name. I'd expected it to feel like an adventure. Instead it felt like... I don't know. A screw-up. A lie.

Then Mabel came in, still smiling nervously, and sat down in the other chair. "Would you like to watch some telly? Or just read? Or we could play a board game?"

I was just considering my options when my phone buzzed in my pocket. Pulling it out, I saw a message from 'Willa' (Alice had insisted that we use each other's names in our phones, just in case).

Have emailed dossier. Get me yours soon?

Which would have been useful say, two hours ago, before dinner.

Of course, I hadn't even started mine, so maybe I should be getting on with that.

Plus, I had plans to make. I'd made it to London against the odds, and it hadn't even involved me running away from my mystery aunt at Heathrow and setting off some sort of girl-hunt across London (which would have made a great story, but 'wanted' posters with my face on them would have made it hard to be anonymous at the theatre). Now I was here, I had more work to do.

I needed to figure out a way to escape from Mabel three days a week to attend the theatre course. It didn't start until next Monday, so I had a few days. I was pretty sure something would show up – I mean, fate had worked its magic to get me to London in the first place. That should have been the hardest part.

Still, it wouldn't hurt to double check my registration online, and check in with the message group that had been set up so we could all get to know each other before the course started. I'd given my name as Willa Martyn, which was my mum's maiden name. I didn't want anyone claiming I'd only got in because I was Scott and Sarra Andrews' daughter. (Not that they would, once they saw me in action, I was sure. My audition video had been *awesome*. One of the crew from Mum's show had helped me film it on set.)

Anyway, there was still stuff to do, was the point. And I couldn't do all that with Mabel looking over my shoulder or asking what I was doing on my tablet.

"Actually, I'm still kind of tired." I looked up from my phone and smiled at Mabel, so she'd know I wasn't avoiding her. Much. "Would you mind if I went to my room? I'd like to, uh, unpack and stuff before I go to bed." That sounded better than 'figure out the next stage of my master plan'.

"Of course!" Mabel bounced to her feet again, then grabbed me a glass of water from the filter jug in the fridge, and guided me towards the spare toiletries in the bathroom (like I hadn't brought my own – well, Alice's – anyway). Finally, I shut the door to my room behind me again, and I was alone.

I flopped on to my bed and pulled out my phone, swiping through to open Alice's dossier. I could base mine on hers, right? Then I'd check out the message group.

I yawned again. Time to get to work.

From: **WillaMayAndrews@purpleworld.com**

To: **AliceJWright@mymail.co.uk**

Re: **Dossier**

Hey Alice

Thanks for the profile. Mabel asks LOTS of questions, so I reckon it'll really help.

Um, in case I didn't say earlier, I'm sorry about your mum, by the way. That really sucks.

Here's Everything You Ever Wanted To Know About Willa Andrews (but didn't have time on the plane to ask).

W x

WILLA MAY ANDREWS

Age: 14. Which you already know. My birthday's October 7th (only two months away, so start present planning now!)

Height: 162cm (last time I got measured)

Eye colour: Chocolate brown. Like my dad.

Family: I'm an only child too. My parents always said that one was more than enough when that one child was me. Other than that … you're basically meeting more of my family this week than I ever have. Mum fell out with her parents before I was born, and like I told you, Dad's dad remarried and moved to Italy when he was a teenager and they didn't really speak much after that. I've never even been to Italy, in fact. Anyway, Dad's mum – my granny – died when I was little.

Friends: My friendship group basically imploded this spring, when everything about my dad came out and I might have got a little bit moody. So anyway, they're not worth talking about. But if you need to mention names at all, you can talk about Noemi and Tara.

Interests & Hobbies: Acting, obviously. Shopping. Hanging out with my friends. And I used to do dance, until last year.

History: I was born in Chester, and we've basically lived in Cheshire most of my life, until the LA move this summer.

Medical Information: I have six toes on my left foot. (Kidding. *Obviously* I don't. But I don't have any interesting allergies or conditions to share either.)

Other Information: I like to dress up, so don't be afraid to try out new combinations from my suitcase or whatever. And I *never* go out without make-up, so get practising your brow definition.

ALICE

I crept back down the stairs from my bedroom in the attic the next morning, not yet sure of the rhythms of Sofia's house, or of what I should be doing there. I wasn't even entirely sure about my choice of outfit from Willa's suitcase. I'd tried to play it safe with denim shorts and a top, but the shorts seemed to hang too low on my hips, and the top, with its cutaway shoulders, seemed like something other girls at school wore on weekends, but I always assumed would look stupid on me. Like I was trying too hard.

The worst part though, by far, was Willa's underwear. Instead of the white, cotton, stretchy crop-top bras I had, or even the one or two proper ones, Willa had packed hot pink, purple, and even zebra print, plunge-style push-up bras with padding – and I had nowhere near enough to fill them.

They looked awful, even under my clothes. I wanted to grab my own bra – even if I had been wearing it for two days and thousands of miles – but

Sofia had already whisked all my travelling clothes away to be washed.

So, it looked like it had to be Willa's bras.

I chose the least baggy one, but even then I could feel it gaping around my chest.

I'd put a white, lacy cardigan over the red top and hoped it didn't look too ridiculous.

Willa had sent her dossier over late the night before, even by UK time, and I'd read it in bed that morning – thankful for the Wi-Fi code Luca had reeled off to me from memory after supper. It didn't really tell me much more than I'd learned on the plane – except maybe that Willa seemed lonelier than I'd expected a girl like her to be. She was so beautiful, so confident, I'd imagined she'd have friends and family across the globe, just waiting to spend time with her.

Which I supposed she did, in a way, since as I reached the bottom of the stairs, Rosa popped into the kitchen doorway and beamed at me.

"Willa's up!" she bellowed, surprisingly loudly for such a small girl. "*Now* can we go out? *Please?*"

Sofia's face appeared behind her, smiling. "Do you not think Willa might want some breakfast first, Rosa?" she asked gently.

"She can eat on the way to the village." Luca pushed

past them both, a bag slung over his shoulder and an apple in his hand. "Catch!" He tossed the apple at me, and I blinked quickly before reaching out to catch it.

Luca grinned. "Good reflexes. And I've muffins in the bag. Come on."

I looked at Sofia for permission, and with a small shrug, she nodded. Apparently I was leaving with Luca and Rosa. I glanced back over my shoulder, wondering where Antonio was this morning.

"Where are we going?" I asked, as we started down the track away from the farmhouse. Even though it was still early, the sun was already hot and high in the sky, tracking its way over the olive groves we'd driven through the day before.

"Well, there *is* a choice," Luca told me. "Beach or town."

I knew which one *I'd* choose – beach, every time. Except I wasn't being Alice today. And Willa – with her love of cities and shopping – would definitely pick the town. But her family probably wouldn't know that, right?

Before I could answer, Luca carried on talking. "But Sofia said your dad told her you're a city girl, so you'll probably want to go see the shops and stuff first, right?"

So much for the beach.

"Right. Town would definitely be my choice," I lied, and Luca nodded.

"OK," he said. Rosa looked disappointed, though.

"But maybe … we could do the beach another day?" Rosa perked up at my suggestion. "I'd like to explore all around here. I've never been to Italy before." At least, I knew now that Willa hadn't. I'd have to be careful not to slip up and mention my last Italian holiday.

Luca shrugged. "We can do that. The harbour is pretty cool."

"But the gelato is better in town," Rosa admitted.

The sun was warm across my back as we passed the gate marking the end of Sofia and Mattias's property and started climbing the hill towards the village I could see perched at the top. The stone houses gleamed in the morning light.

"Do you like living with Sofia and Mattias?" I asked, as we walked. I figured there was no point avoiding the topic of their foster care.

Rosa nodded emphatically. "I love Sofia. And Mattias, even though he can't cook."

Luca took a moment longer to answer. "They're very kind," he said slowly. "And I like the farm. I like helping with the animals."

Rosa had mentioned chickens last night, I remembered. "But I thought Antonio said it was an olive farm?" I tried not to blush as I said his name, and remembered him meeting my gaze for a second in the rear-view mirror as he drove and Sofia talked.

I *knew* Antonio was too old for me, and even though he'd been friendly, it wasn't as if he'd been flirting with me or anything. So why couldn't I stop thinking about him? And *blushing*, of all the ridiculous things.

Maybe trying to Be More Willa was affecting my brain.

"There are olive groves too," Luca replied, oblivious. "But Sofia loves animals. And she says that if you live somewhere like this, it's only right to keep some. So there are chickens, a goat, a cow for milk, that sort of thing. Oh, and the sheepdog. Even though there aren't any sheep."

"But there are cats! You mustn't forget the cats!" Rosa put in. "Mattias says they're the 'most overpaid mouse catchers in Italy'."

I laughed. "Your English is so good, Rosa. And yours too, of course, Luca."

"We're half English," Luca reminded me. "Our father only ever spoke English to us. So we had to learn."

There was something in his tone, something darker that told me not to ask any more questions.

I looked away. "Well, I'm sorry I don't speak any Italian. But I'm a quick learner, and I love languages. So maybe you two can teach me?" Too late, I remembered that *Alice* loved languages, not Willa.

Luca and Rosa wouldn't know that, but I *had* to remember to Be More Willa. I couldn't be sure how much Sofia and the others already knew about her – her dad had told them about her love of towns over beaches, after all. How much more had he told them? Probably more than he'd told Willa about *them*, I was guessing.

Rosa linked her arm through mine, skipping a little to keep up with me. "I can teach you Italian. First we'll learn 'Good morning'. That's *Buongiorno*. Say *Buongiorno*."

"*Buongiorno*," I echoed, purposefully badly enough to make Rosa sigh heavily.

"This is going to take a while," she said.

Luca and I exchanged a look, and he smirked, just a bit.

"I reckon I need to be able to order a gelato in Italian by the time we reach the village, right?" I said.

"Definitely," Luca agreed. "Better get to work, Rosa."

Rosa gave me a long-suffering look. "I think you'd better learn to order *three* gelatos."

"Fair enough," I said, with a laugh. "So teach me."

The walk to the village of Tusello took another ten minutes or so, by which time I could manage a passable gelato order, much to Rosa's delight. But instead of taking us straight to the gelato shop – which didn't open until eleven, Rosa informed me, the minute I'd mastered the phrase – Luca took us on a tour of the village.

For someone who'd only been living there eighteen months, Luca had clearly made it his mission to learn every nook and cranny of the place. He led us confidently through *piazzas* – small squares where many roads through the village met and pastel-coloured houses with wrought-iron balconies looked out over benches and trees and tiny, dark shops that sold everything. He took us past cafés with people sitting outside them sipping coffee, and ancient churches and monuments. But when I asked about the history of the buildings we saw, he just shrugged.

"I like to know where all the paths and roads go,"

was all he said. "The rest of it isn't important. Come on, the gelato shop should be open by now."

He hopped down from the low wall we were sitting on, watching people go by, and headed across the street and down another alleyway that – I was almost sure – led back to the main piazza.

Rosa slipped her hand into mine as we followed him. "We've lived in a lot of places," she said, quietly enough that Luca, paces ahead of us, wouldn't hear. "Luca always goes out investigating when we end up somewhere new. It's so he can find the best escape routes And hiding places. He likes trees best for that. He can climb higher than anyone, even Antonio."

Which made me wonder about what circumstances had led Luca, Rosa and Antonio to be placed with Sofia and Mattias. As I watched Luca's dark hair shining in the sun, and his shoulders hunched over as he darted past cars, I got the feeling they must have been really bad.

Whatever those circumstances were, I knew I'd never ask Luca. But maybe, if we became friends, he'd tell me in his own time.

Even if I could never tell him the truth about my own family.

"Now, say it one more time for practice," Rosa

instructed, as we reached the piazza. "And remember, I want strawberry."

"*Fragola,*" I said, remembering.

"See?" Luca said. "She's ready. Come on, let's order. Then we can go eat them by the walls."

Rosa only had to help me once with the ordering (I got confused by a question about cones or cups) but soon we had our three gelatos (strawberry for Rosa, pistachio for me and vanilla for Luca) and were heading back through shaded side streets.

"So, why haven't you ever visited Sofia and Mattias before?" Luca asked, catching me by surprise as I savoured my pistachio gelato. "I mean, you're their niece, right? But Sofia said she'd never even met you before yesterday."

I took a large bite of gelato, hoping that having my mouth full would give me long enough to try to remember the details from Willa's dossier. Mostly it just made my teeth hurt, though.

"Ow! Ow, ow, ow," I moaned around the gelato.

"Sensitive teeth," Rosa said sagely. "Antonio has that problem. You should lick, not bite."

"Right." I swallowed down the gelato. Now I had an ice-cream headache, and still didn't have a good answer for Luca.

He was waiting for one, though. My show with the gelato hadn't distracted him from his question at all.

"Um, I … don't really know why," I said honestly. "My dad never talked about Sofia. She's his half-sister, you see." At least I remembered that much. "I don't think they really even knew each other growing up. They've only recently got back in touch."

All true, for Willa, at least as far as I could remember. But I wasn't sure that Luca was completely sold on my answer.

Finally, we popped out of the dark alleyways into blazing sunlight.

"We're here," Rosa said delightedly, hopping forwards to sit against the perimeter wall that Luca had promised me was the best place to eat ice cream.

It was a little tumbledown in places, but I wasn't looking at the crumbling masonry. I was looking beyond it – down the hill, away from the village and out to sea.

The Tyrrhenian Sea sparkled in the sunlight, glittering all the way out to where it joined the

Mediterranean. (I'd studied maps of the area around Sofia's farm on my phone, waiting for the plane in London, so I at least knew the names of the places I'd be seeing. I hadn't been able to spot Mum's waterfall, though.) Below us, I could see the harbour, along with a row of hotels and restaurants and shops that bordered a sandy white beach, which ran all the way to the rocky cliffs that marked the end of the cove.

"It's beautiful." I breathed in the salt air, breezing up from the ocean, and instantly felt at home.

Luca was watching me carefully. "There's caves at the end of the beach. One of them even has a mini waterfall running through it from some underground stream. It's small, but kind of cool."

The one Mum had wanted to see – that she claimed could set all your worries free – could never be called 'mini', so it couldn't be the same one. But it was still a waterfall.

I smiled. I'd definitely made the right choice, being Willa this summer.

"Your gelato is melting," Rosa pointed out.

I stopped staring out to sea and licked the edge of my cone before it started dripping on to my already sticky hands.

We finished our gelatos in silence, our backs against

the medieval wall, looking across at the village that Luca and Rosa called home, for now.

As we started back down the winding path round the hill, Rosa skipped ahead, finding wildflowers on the edge of the road and coloured stones to store in her pockets.

Luca walked beside me, both of us watching her go.

"Why didn't you pick the beach this morning?" he asked, after a moment. When I shot him a confused look, he raised his eyebrows. "I saw you looking out at it. You looked like you were ... longing for it. I wouldn't have thought a city girl like you would look like that."

Oops. I'd let myself be Alice, instead of Willa, just for a few minutes. I couldn't afford to do that again. Especially around Luca, it seemed. Apparently paths and hiding places weren't the only things he paid close attention to. He was perceptive about people too.

I'd have to be careful to *always* be Willa around Luca.

"I can't like both? Besides, Rosa said the best gelato was in the town," I said lightly, hoping he didn't remember that she'd said it *after* I'd chosen the town. "And I *really* wanted gelato this morning."

"Right." Luca didn't look convinced but he didn't ask any more questions.

Which was just as well, as I didn't have any answers. At least, not ones I could share with him.

WILLA

"I'm really so sorry about this," Mabel said for, like, the fourteenth time since breakfast. "It really shouldn't take me too long to finish and then we can do something else. After lunch at the latest."

She stopped walking suddenly and I had to backtrack a couple of steps until I saw the plaque on the building she'd halted at. *Queen Anne's University, London.*

I'd checked out the university Mabel worked at online the night before, and it hadn't looked like this. The photos on the website were of an imposing building with columns and steps.

This place had no columns. It just had, well, bricks. And a plaque.

"Back entrance," Mabel said, picking up on my look. "I promise the place is more impressive from the front, but I tend to get collared by research students who haven't gone home for the summer. Much easier to get in and out this way, if I'm in a hurry."

Sneaky.

Mabel had been mortified that she'd been called into work on my first day, but actually I didn't mind so much. It meant she'd be distracted, for a start, so wouldn't ask so many questions about my life or my *feelings* (which was even worse). As far as I was concerned, feelings were for sharing with friends, and maybe boyfriends. Not someone else's sort-of stepmother. Especially since the feelings she wanted to discuss were *Alice's* anyway.

No, thank you. Far too complicated.

So I figured I'd explore the uni a bit while she worked, maybe find some people to chat to. Hopefully something would show up to help with my plan to escape to attend my theatre course next week. If Mabel was going to be working a lot, that could help…

Or maybe I'd just study Alice's dossier again, to try to get the answers for the next lot of questions. It wasn't like there was really a whole lot of information in the thing, just the basics. But it *sounded* like Alice, and that was what I needed most. I'd spent less than a day with her and, even though I'd tried to pay attention, I was already starting to forget the details. Her expressions, her way of speaking, how she fiddled with her hair. Even holding on to her accent – which wasn't very different to mine, before I'd spent a few weeks in America – was a struggle.

Reading something she'd written helped. Which gave me an idea.

Pulling my phone from my pocket I tapped out a quick message to Alice as I followed Mabel up the narrow staircase and into a long corridor lined with closed doors, each with a small brass nameplate.

How's Italy? I typed, then waited to see it was delivered. No blue tick to tell me it had been read, though, so I shoved the phone back in my pocket. She'd get it eventually, then we could chat. Even text chat would be better than nothing, and we'd agreed it was important we stay in close contact while we were pretending to be each other.

"Here we are." Mabel stopped in front of one of the many doors and slipped a key into the lock. "My home away from home."

Mabel's office felt a lot like her flat. There were books everywhere, especially on the big wooden desk under the window. There was an armchair in the corner, and a fish tank on one of the shelves. I peered closer at it. Were those *starfish*?

Catching me looking, Mabel smiled. "Your dad gave them to me, in case you hadn't guessed."

I hadn't but I probably should have done.

Mabel shifted a stack of books off the armchair and motioned for me to sit. "I just need to go and speak with a colleague of mine for a moment. Will you be OK here on your own?"

"Yeah, of course." I waved my phone at her. "I wanted to check Instagram anyway."

Alice had refused point blank to take over my Instagram account while she was pretending to be me, which was probably for the best. I doubted she'd keep up my carefully chosen palette anyway. Although it would be nice to share some photos of Italy to show off my supposed summer there... Maybe I'd work on her again when she was a bit more settled in. I didn't want to lose my audience.

And in the meantime, at least I could check my notifications.

"I'll be back as soon as I can," Mabel said, and then with the same flustered, flapping movements she used around me, she left. The door stayed half open behind her.

Maybe it wasn't just Alice's visit making her nervous. Maybe she was just like that?

I'd barely scrolled through half my social-media updates when there was a sharp knock on the door. Whoever it was clearly had no manners because they didn't wait to be asked in.

"Professor Jennings? Tim said he saw you sneaking in. My dad sent me to ask—" The boy in the doorway stopped, blinked, then pointed a stack of papers at me. "OK, you're not Professor Jennings."

"You don't say." I met his gaze and stared back at him. He looked about my age, and kind of cute in a geeky way, with thick-rimmed tortoiseshell glasses and black hair flopping over one eye. Not my type, but I could imagine him being Alice's.

"So? Who are you?" He didn't stop long enough to let me answer, just kept looking at me like I was a puzzle to solve. "You're too young to be a student, and Professor Jennings doesn't have kids. A niece, maybe? Goddaughter?"

"I'm Alice Wright." The name came off my tongue more smoothly than I'd thought it would. "Mabel's a … friend of my dad's and I'm staying with her for the summer."

Easy. I was great at this acting thing.

"You're not Alice." The boy was pointing an accusatory finger at me this time. "I *know* Alice Wright, and you're *definitely* not her."

Oh hell.

Before I could come up with an explanation, Mabel

bustled back in. "Hal! I see you already found Alice. Wait, you two know each other, don't you? I'm sure your dad said—"

"Absolutely!" I jumped in, hoping Hal would go along with my lie. "Actually, Hal was just offering to give me a tour of the university. Weren't you?" I stared at him, hard, and willed him to say the right thing.

"Uh, yeah. I guess I was." There was a confused line between his eyebrows, but he'd gone along with it. I unclenched my jaw, just a little.

"Oh, brilliant!" Mabel said. "Because I think I'm going to be stuck here a little longer than I thought. Just text me when you're on your way back, Alice, and I'll meet you out front so we can head home together." Then she frowned again. "Wait, is that what your dad would say?"

"Absolutely." I edged towards the doorway, more than ready to make my escape. "Word for word. I'll see you later!"

Grabbing Hal's hand, I dragged him out of the door behind me, letting it bang shut after us. All the air in my lungs whooshed out with relief.

"Mind telling me what all that was about? And, uh, maybe let go of my hand?"

I dropped his hand quickly. *Super* embarrassing.

"We should find somewhere to talk that isn't the middle of a corridor. It's kind of a long story."

Hal looked at me like he was assessing my crazy level. I tried to look sane.

"OK," he said, after a moment. "Um, did you really want the tour?"

"I'd rather have an iced coffee," I said, with a bright smile. "Does this place have a coffee shop?"

"Uh, yeah. I think there's one in the quad." He started down the corridor, the opposite way to where I'd come in, and I followed, thinking hard. Just because Hal hadn't told Mabel I wasn't Alice, didn't mean he wouldn't later. Unless I could convince him to go along with my act.

That was going to take more than acting. That was going to take diplomacy. And I'd never been very good at that.

"So let me get this straight," Hal said, his hands wrapped round his drink. "Alice is in Italy pretending to be you, and you're here in London pretending to be Alice."

I glanced around the courtyard, making sure that

none of the other people sitting outside the coffee shop in the sunshine were listening. Luckily they all seemed more interested in their own conversations. Which was their loss, really. Ours was *far* better. "That's about it."

Hal shook his head, like he was a disappointed head teacher rather than a, what, fourteen-year-old guy? "I just can't see the Alice Wright I know skipping off to Italy and lying to everyone. Especially not her dad. It's just so ... irresponsible. And Alice, well, isn't. She's kind and thoughtful and..." He looked down at the table and shrugged. "I just can't see it."

Hmm. Seemed to me he thought very highly of our Alice... "Alice said ... what was it? Right. Death or glory, think of the story."

That made him laugh. "OK, that sounds a lot more like Jon than Alice."

"Jon? Who's Jon? She said it was something her dad used to say."

Hal gave me a sideways look. "Alice's dad *is* Jon. Didn't you two prepare for this charade at all?"

I winced. "It was kind of a last-minute decision. We only had the flight to figure everything out. And then Alice sent me this dossier, but it's hard to remember it all." Hal was looking suspicious again.

Like he thought I'd forced Alice into the swap – when technically, it was actually her idea. "I'm pretty sure she mentioned you though… Remind me, how do you two know each other?"

Best way to get information out of someone – pretend you already know the answer. Works with teachers, parents, and definitely with boys who have a crush. And I was almost certain that Hal had a *big* one on Alice.

The suspicion on Hal's face was replaced by something else. "Alice talked about me? Or wrote about me? What did she say?"

Definitely a crush. "Oh, you know. Usual stuff. Tell me how you guys met and it might jog my memory…"

"Oh, my dad used to work with Alice's dad at the university up in Cambridge. Although my dad's biochemistry, not marine biology. Anyway, we met at their first university family function after they moved there a couple of years ago. Then my stupid parents got divorced and Dad moved down to Queen Anne's last September. I haven't seen Alice since."

"Well, now her dad's dating Mabel, I bet you'll be seeing a lot more of her." Apart from the fact I was supposed to be putting Mabel off. But Hal didn't need to know that.

"You'll tell her I'm here?" Hal asked eagerly.

"Absolutely. She'll be thrilled that we're hanging out, I'm sure."

"We're hanging out, now?" Hal raised his eyebrows. "Like, again?"

"Well, as you pointed out, Alice and I haven't had time to iron out all the kinks in our plan. Someone who can vouch for me as Alice could be invaluable…"

"It does sound like you're going to need some help," Hal conceded.

Bingo. "So you'll help me?"

"I didn't say that," Hal hedged, but it was too late.

"You implied it. It would be rude not to help me now."

"Rude?"

I nodded emphatically. "Absolutely. I'm a lost soul, wandering the streets of London. More than that, I'm a friend of a friend. You should totally give me your number so we can make plans. It's, like, your friend obligation to help me."

"Friend obligation? I thought you *just* met Alice. You didn't even remember her dad's name."

"I spent ten whole hours on a flight with her. Plus, you know, agreed to swap summers with her. If that doesn't make us friends, I don't know what does."

"It definitely doesn't make it any less insane," Hal mumbled.

"Maybe not. But you're going to help me anyway, right?" Time to bring out my best card. "I know Alice would really, really appreciate it if you did."

Hal sighed. I knew that sigh. That was a sigh of giving in to my overwhelming persistence. I'd heard it plenty of times before from other people, but I wasn't sure I'd ever been quite so relieved by the sound.

"One condition," Hal said, holding up a finger. "You have to tell me your real name."

I glanced around again to make sure no one was listening, then leaned in across the table and whispered. "Willa Andrews. But you *have* to call me Alice, whenever anyone else might hear. Deal?"

"Deal." He sounded resigned. "But I'm almost certain I'm going to regret this."

WILLA

How's Italy?

WILLA

Never mind Italy. Why the hell didn't you warn me about Hal?

ALICE

The gelato is amazing. As long as you don't eat it too quick. And Hal who?

ALICE

Hang on. Hal Asato? Dad's friend's son?

ALICE

What's he doing in London?

ALICE

Wait, they moved there, right? After the divorce. How could I forget that?

ALICE

Oh my God, Willa.

ALICE

This is a disaster!

ALICE

You have to stay away from him. He'll definitely know you're not me.

ALICE

Oh God, does he know Mabel too? Why didn't I think of that?

ALICE

Has he told her? What's happening?!?!

ALICE

WILLA!!

WILLA

OK, chill. All dealt with. I've filled him in on our swap and he's on our side.

WILLA

Well, he won't tell Mabel anyway.

WILLA

I think he thinks it's kind of funny. Or insane.

WILLA

Maybe both.

ALICE

He's not wrong...

ALICE

It's really OK?

WILLA

It's fine.

WILLA

You can stop hyperventilating now.

WILLA

Actually, I think he has a crush on you.

ALICE

Don't be ridiculous.

WILLA

It's kind of cute.

WILLA

So, tell me about Italy?

ALICE

OK. But settle in, because there's lot to tell.

And then I want to hear all about London...

ALICE

The next morning, as I dug through Willa's clothes to try to find something more 'me', I realized my mistake.

I wasn't Being More Willa if I played it safe with the outfits, activities and conversations. If I wanted to experience Willa's confidence and self-assurance, I had to act as if I already had them.

Willa had got me to tell her all about my mum dying and my dad sending me to stay with his new girlfriend within hours of meeting me – and that was before you got into the whole swapping summer thing. She'd *definitely* have asked Luca or Antonio why they were living with Sofia by now.

Willa would have wanted to do more than just eat ice cream in Tusello – she'd have made friends with the locals and probably found herself invited to some party or other.

And most of all, she'd wear whatever she wanted to wear – and she wouldn't worry if anyone else thought it looked stupid.

Since I didn't have the courage (yet) to ask Luca

about his family, or the Italian to get invited to parties, I decided to start my Be More Willa campaign with today's outfit.

I purposefully chose the brightest, flashiest bra in the drawer and, when it didn't fit (obviously) I stuffed the cups with a couple of spare socks to make it look less empty. Next, I chose a bright red top and a white, tiered skirt that I would never normally have worn.

When I looked in the mirror, I barely recognized myself, as I parted my hair on the wrong side and pulled it into a low plait that hung over one shoulder. (I didn't attempt the Dutch braid Willa had done for me on the plane, but it looked pretty good anyway.)

Very Willa.

I skipped down the stairs to the kitchen, only to bump into Antonio coming out the other way, carrying a bag full of apples. Three of them went rolling across the floor.

"Sorry!" I dropped to my knees, my face probably the colour of Willa's top, and tried to gather up the apples. My first opportunity to talk to Antonio with Willa's confidence, and I ruined it.

"Don't worry about it." Antonio kneeled beside me, reaching under a cabinet to try to retrieve the last apple.

"I'll get it." I shuffled closer, and my hand brushed against his as I stretched out my fingers. My cheeks got hotter. Antonio, of course, was completely unaffected.

Finally, my hand closed round the apple and I pulled it out. I held it in my palm as I started to get up from the floor, and he reached to take it from me.

Which was when it happened. The most embarrassing moment of my life to date.

As I leaned forwards, my top moved forwards too. And so did Willa's stupid bra.

The socks I'd stuffed it with tumbled to the ground.

My face burning, I bit the inside of my cheek to keep from crying.

Antonio had dropped the apple again in the effort of trying not to laugh. He bent over to pick it up, and I heard a muffled snicker from him as he did so. Apparently my humiliation was just *too* funny.

I could feel my chest tightening as my breath grew shallow. I *couldn't* lose it now, though. I had to be Willa.

So what would Willa do?

The answer pinged into my head instantly. She'd carry on as if nothing had happened. She wouldn't *let* herself care.

So neither would I.

It took all my courage – and several deep breaths – but then, as casually as I could, I picked up the socks, clutched them in my hand so tightly you couldn't even see them, and stood up.

"Enjoy the apples," I said, looking straight at Antonio. (OK, I was actually looking somewhere over his left shoulder, but it was a start!) And then I walked, slowly, past him and out of the front door. I didn't let myself run until I was sure he couldn't see.

I stashed the socks behind a plant pot by the door, and headed out to explore more of the farm. By the time I bumped into Mattias coming along the path with a goat beside him, my cheeks were probably more fuchsia than flame red, which was a start.

"Are you looking for Luca?" he asked.

"Uh, yes." I hadn't been, but it seemed as good an idea as any.

"I think he was headed to the stables." Mattias jerked his head towards the wooden structures just beside the path.

"Great. Thanks." I gave him what I suspected

was an unconvincing smile. I'd never liked horses, not since an unfortunate riding party for a friend's birthday when we were eight. One of the horses had smelled the mints in my pocket and chewed halfway through my jacket to get them – and taken a chomp of my elbow too.

I'd avoided horses ever since. Until now.

Because now, Luca had appeared in the door of the barn next to the stables and was waving at me, and Mattias was smiling indulgently, waiting for me to run and join him.

Did Willa like horses? I had no idea. But I couldn't rule out the possibility that she'd been riding in gymkhanas since she was three and her dad had told Sofia and her family all about it.

I'd used up pretty much all my courage dealing with the bra incident, but it seemed I was going to have to find some more.

"You didn't mention the horses in your list of animals." I gazed nervously at the stables as I approached.

Luca glanced back at me as he made his way inside, a bucket in hand. "They're not horses. And believe me, they're going to be a lot more scared of you than you are of them."

"I'm not scared," I lied. "Just … cautious."

Luca didn't answer that.

Warily, I stepped forwards, following him into the stables. The scent of the hay and the animals sent me straight back to that eighth birthday party.

Luca raised the bucket of food he'd carried from the barn and emptied it into the trough at the front of the stable. I stopped breathing altogether as I waited for the thunder of hooves…

A thin grey donkey trotted out and stuck its muzzle in the trough. Behind it came an even smaller donkey, this one dragging one of its back legs.

OK, even I couldn't be scared of these two. Much.

"They were going to be put down because no one wanted them, but Sofia saved them. She can't resist rescuing lost and abandoned creatures." Luca leaned against the wall of the stable beside me, watching the donkeys eat. "I think that's why she took me and my brother and sister in, really."

"You're not lame donkeys," I pointed out. "It's kind of different."

Luca shrugged. "Not really. No one else wanted us either."

He pushed away from the wall, as if he'd said too much, and went to pet the lame donkey's ears instead.

"This one is Achilles," he told me, without looking up. "The other is Hercules."

"Big names for little donkeys."

"Sofia has high hopes for things. Even lame donkeys."

I thought about what Luca had said as I followed him around the rest of the farmyard, putting out food and water for the animals. Every one of them seemed to have a rescue story – even the chickens.

"The old farmer down the road was selling up," Luca explained, as he felt around in the straw for an egg. "The chickens would have been killed, I guess, if he couldn't find another home for them. So Sofia declared that eggs for breakfast were her favourite thing and moved them here. Mattias said she'd never eaten eggs in the morning before then."

We delivered the eggs to Sofia in the kitchen, where Rosa was sat at the big, battered wooden table practising her reading, and were rewarded with muffins, still warm from the oven.

"Come on," Luca said. "We can eat them outside."

I felt almost guilty, sitting in the sunshine with Luca, under the sparse shade of an olive grove, biting into the most delicious blueberry muffin I'd ever tasted. I wasn't supposed to be here, enjoying all this

– Willa was. If she'd known how warm and happy Sofia's house was, would she still have picked London? I couldn't know.

We'd texted until almost midnight the night before, filling each other in on our adventures so far. Willa seemed to be having fun planning and scheming in London – at least, after the near disaster of bumping into Hal. I'd totally forgotten he'd even moved to London (in fact, I'd not really thought about him over the last year) but I was glad she had someone on her side, at least.

Just like I had Luca for company. I watched him from under my lashes, as he sat beside me in companionable silence while we were eating. Did he really think he was as lost and as broken as those poor donkeys? What had happened to the rest of his family to make him feel that way? Antonio and Rosa both seemed confident and happy – or was that just a show? Maybe they were all as insecure as Luca, but he was just more honest about it.

"So, if your dad and Sofia never really knew each other, how come you're here now?" Luca asked.

I tensed up for a second before realizing I had all the answers to that question. What worried me more was that he'd clearly been thinking about it since our conversation yesterday, if he was bringing it up again now.

I tried to channel Willa's feelings and gave him a sad smile. "I'm like Achilles and Hercules. No one wanted me this summer, either. Dad's in Edinburgh performing at the Fringe, Mum's in LA filming, and they're both far too busy with their acting careers to have me there with them. Sofia was the only person who wanted me."

It was Willa's story, not mine, but it felt true all the same.

"So you're another of Sofia's lost souls, then?" Luca said, looking at me with new interest. "Guess we've got something more in common than a love of gelato after all."

"I guess so."

We held each other's gazes for a moment, then looked away again, both turning our attention back to our muffins. But I hid a small smile as I bit into mine.

WILLA

"I thought you were going to unpack the other night?" Mabel looked confused as she took in the state of my bedroom – previously her office.

I tried to see it through her eyes. The desk was covered in chargers and headphones and the couple of magazines I'd grabbed from my bag before handing it to Alice. Yesterday's clothes were piled on the chair, and my shoes were scattered somewhere underneath. And in the middle of the tiny floor space was Alice's suitcase, open and overflowing, but obviously not in any way unpacked.

"I, uh, guess I was too tired," I lied. Actually, I just hated unpacking (doesn't everybody?) and besides, I'd had to type up my profile for Alice on my tablet. And since then I … just hadn't really wanted to.

"Would you like me to help?" Mabel glanced between the suitcase and the empty clothes rail. For someone who had no problems with books taking over every surface in her house, she was kind of particular about clothes clutter, it seemed.

"Nah, I'll do it." Pushing myself up off the bed, I kneeled next to Alice's suitcase and started pulling out items. And pulling faces.

So far, I'd managed to put up with the 'jeans and T-shirt' look that Alice preferred, but I had to admit, I'd been hoping there might be something a little more interesting buried in the case that I'd somehow missed when rummaging through it.

No such luck. Apparently the clothes Alice had been wearing on the plane had been the height of her fashion styling. Which was to say, about the height of a small kitten.

"If you're sure…" Mabel gave one last meaningful look at the clothes rail, then disappeared. I waited until I heard the kettle click on in the kitchen – the woman was *addicted* to tea – then whipped out my phone to text Alice. We'd made plans to message each other with updates later that night, after we'd gone to bed and were safely alone, but this actually couldn't wait.

Seriously. What's with your clothes?

No response.

To prove my point, I collected some of the most offensive items (baggy T-shirt with 'Ask me about marine biology' on the front with a picture of some fish;

a 'Live life on porpoise' vest top; baggy cargo shorts with pockets *everywhere*; and a dress with roses on that looked like a five-year-old girl's best party outfit) and took photos to send to Alice to accompany my message above.

Still no answer.

Sighing, I began categorizing the contents of the suitcase as I hung them up or put them away in the drawer Mabel had cleared for me in the chest by the door.

Category 1: Basics I could wear – plain fitted T-shirts, jeans, etc.

Category 2: Items I could make interesting – a pair of denim cut-offs that could probably be cut off a little bit more. A maxi skirt that could definitely work with a crop top – if I could find one.

Category 3: Things I was going to pretend I'd never seen, for the sake of my eyes – almost everything else.

Categories 4–5 were underwear and socks, shoes and accessories. (Huge surprise, Alice hadn't embraced the importance of accessorizing. That was probably the smallest category. In my world, you weren't properly dressed without earrings and a bag – preferably designer. I wasn't even sure Alice *had* her ears pierced.)

The rest of the suitcase, to my horror, was full of books. As if the three in her hand luggage hadn't been enough.

Haven't you ever heard of an e-reader? I texted, as I stacked the books on top of Mabel's on the desk.

Once everything was put away, I sank down on the bed again and stared accusingly at the clothes rail. It wasn't like I thought clothes were the *most* important thing on the planet. Just maybe the second or third.

I *liked* clothes. I liked picking an outfit to suit my mood. I liked choosing the perfect belt to go with a dress, or finding a pair of jeans that fitted just right. My mum always said that our clothes were our character on show.

Which was the problem. I wasn't Willa right now – I was Alice.

But maybe Alice had just never learned about fashion. Maybe this would be the summer that 'Alice' would discover a new love of style.

Because there was no way in hell I was wearing that child's party dress.

I decided to embrace the next few weeks as a fashion challenge. Crossing to the clothes rail, I ran my fingers over the fabrics, trying to visualize a few not-hideous outfits I could create from what I had to work with. Maybe I could cut off the bottom of that red tank and make it into a crop top…

"Alice?" I spun round to find Mabel in the doorway again. "Oh, this looks much better! And you've got your books out. That will make you feel more at home, I'm sure. I always feel more settled once I've unpacked my books."

"Yeah, of course." For me, that would normally be my make-up. Alice barely had any. All I'd found in her wash bag was some tinted lip balm and clear mascara. No bronzer, no brow palette, no fake lashes … nothing. I felt naked without it. But I figured that even Mabel would know Alice wasn't exactly the YouTube-beauty-contouring type, so I'd have to tone down my usual style even when I got to go shopping for supplies.

Mabel sank down on to the bed, smiling as she looked around the room. It wasn't *tidy* exactly, but it looked like someone was living there – not just passing through. Maybe that was what she liked about it.

"It was nice that you got to see Hal at the university yesterday. Your dad mentioned that the two of you were friends."

"Yeah, I guess." An idea started to form. "Um, actually we were planning to try to hang out some more next week. Maybe a few days, if that's OK with you?"

If I could get Hal to act as my alibi, this could be the solution to the theatre course!

To my surprise, Mabel looked relieved. "Actually, that would be perfect. It looks like I might have to spend a few days at work next week, unfortunately, and I'd hate for you to be stuck there bored. But if you're hanging out with Hal I'll worry much less."

"Brilliant! Uh, not that you have to work, of course. But it'll be nice to spend time with Hal." I remembered what he'd said about his dad moving. "I haven't seen him since they moved to London last September." It's always the true details that make a lie convincing.

"Good. But I was also wondering … your dad mentioned you might like to go shopping? He actually sent some money for me to take you to pick up new clothes or whatever you might need. I don't know much about teen fashions these days, but I can't be any worse at it than your dad would be. I was thinking maybe we could go to the Westfield shopping centre tomorrow? Make the most of our first weekend together?"

I couldn't help myself. I launched myself at Mabel and hugged her hard.

Mabel laughed. "I'll take that as a yes, then?"

"Take that as a 'definitely'."

Not only was I going to be able to make my theatre course, but my prayers to the fashion gods had been answered! I pulled out my phone to text Hal and make plans for next week. This summer was going to be *awesome*.

ALICE

I wasn't sure if it was the time zone changes still affecting my body clock, or the warm Italian sun streaming through my picture window, but I kept waking up early. Well, not as early as Mattias, who started work on the farm at sunrise, but before Luca and the others at least.

Back home, I loved a holiday lie-in – my dad would have to come and drag me from my bed to go out on adventures with him. But here, I found myself awake early every morning.

The extra time was good, actually. I'd started scribbling in my journal – writing about what we'd been doing, things I'd learned about Sofia and her family, including Luca and his brother and sister. I wrote a *lot* about how everything felt (the incident with Antonio and the bra socks had taken up three whole pages) and I always felt better for seeing it down on paper. Given how much had happened in the last few days, I knew I was at risk of getting overwhelmed and anxious again. So I did what I knew worked to keep me calm.

Then I'd hide my journal under my mattress, just in case anyone went snooping, and head down to join the others for breakfast. It was my new routine, and I liked it.

But when I woke up on Saturday morning, something was different.

There was the most amazing smell wafting up the stairs from the kitchen. Something sharp and sweet and citrusy. Pushing off the blankets, I quickly washed and dressed then headed to the kitchen to find out exactly what it was.

"Ah, good! My next helper." Sofia shot me a wicked smile as I loitered in the kitchen doorway.

"I just wanted to find out what that gorgeous smell was," I admitted.

"That's how she reels them in," Antonio said, grinning as he perched on the kitchen counter. My stomach waged a war between clenched embarrassment and butterflies as I saw him there. One thing me and my journal had definitely decided between us – this crush of mine wasn't nearly as much fun as all the TV shows made it out to be. In fact, most of the time it was just mortifying.

Sofia waved a tray of small cakes in my direction, and

I turned my attention to her, happy for the distraction. "My grandmother's lemon cake recipe. They're waiting to be iced once they cool. But they taste best warm…"

"I love lemon cake," I said, hoping she'd take the hint.

"And you may have one." Beaming, I reached out to take one… "*If* you agree to help me in the kitchen today."

I hadn't baked in years. Oh, I cooked, a little – some simple dishes I'd learned, to help Dad out during busy weeks by making dinner for us both. But baking … that was something Mum and I used to do together. Grandma Wendy too, before she died. Grandma used to joke that sugar was our family tradition.

Bake away your troubles, Alice. Mum's voice was soft but clear in my head. I remembered her telling me that once, after I'd had a huge argument with Claire, back in Year Five. Mum and I had spent the afternoon creating new kinds of cakes – finding the best combinations of flavours and ingredients together. By the time we presented our creations to Dad at teatime, I'd forgotten all about the argument.

Maybe I could bake away my crush on Antonio.

It felt strange, the idea of baking with Sofia, the way I used to with Mum. But nice too, in a way. Nice to remember that not all good things had to go away, just because people did.

And I really did love lemon cake.

Decision made, I took my cake. "OK, then. What are we doing?"

"Tomorrow is the village food festival." Sofia pulled more ingredients from the cupboard below the counter. "Every year, all the locals compete to provide the most delicious food at the stalls."

"Plus there's dancing and music and games," Antonio added. "You'll love it, Willa. I'll show you around all the best stalls."

Sofia cleared her throat and Antonio flashed her a smile.

"Of course, Sofia's food is the absolute greatest," he added.

I barely heard him. I was still stuck on his previous statement. *I'll show you around.*

Was this all it took? I changed my name and my jeans and suddenly I had a gorgeous seventeen-year-old Italian wanting to escort me to a festival? Probably this sort of thing happened to Willa all the time.

Antonio hadn't exactly asked me out on a date – we'd all go together as a family. But that logic didn't change the way it made me feel and I bit the inside of my cheek to keep from smiling.

"Anyway, I have a lot of baking to do, and a reputation to uphold," Sofia went on. "I tested all the recipes the other weekend, but I need a sous chef!"

It turned out that Sofia's new recipes weren't just for cakes. She wanted to make savoury dishes, desserts, sweets and canapés galore.

"What did you do with all the food from the trial run?" I asked, as I leafed through her recipe stack.

Sofia shrugged. "We have two teenage boys in the house – plus Mattias, who is even worse. It all got eaten."

Just then, Mattias passed through the kitchen, snagging a lemon cake as he went. He pressed a quick kiss to the side of Sofia's neck.

"Don't listen to her, Willa. Whenever she does a big cooking weekend, she always gives half the food to the shelter, up in the village." He bit into his cake. "But only half. Me and the boys definitely eat the rest! Come on, Antonio. Work to do!"

Antonio sighed and followed, and then they were gone, back out to do whatever it was olive farmers did all day. I watched them go, thinking about my sort-of date with Antonio tomorrow. If it went well, maybe I'd tell him about Mum's waterfall. Maybe he'd know where it was. Maybe he'd even take me there…

"Luca already told me you can't resist helping lost souls," I said to Sofia. "Like the animals."

"Mattias says I have a good-Samaritan problem." Sofia chuckled. "But the way I see it, I'm so lucky to have my life. Why not share some of that luck?"

"Is that why you agreed to have me stay for the summer?" The question was out before I'd really thought about it.

Sofia gave me a long look, then pushed a kitchen stool towards me. "Sit down, Willa."

I did as I was told, but never took my eyes off Sofia as she pulled up her own stool next to me. Then, apparently as an afterthought, she hopped down, grabbed a tray of freshly baked savoury pastries, and put them on a plate between us before sitting again.

"Your father, he's, I think, thirteen years older than me. I never really knew him growing up, and I only met him a few times after that, to be honest. I think … my mama always said that he didn't deal well with his parents' divorce. And still less well when our father remarried my mother. He visited once, I think, when Mama was pregnant with me, but it didn't go well."

"So you don't really know him at all." And yet Willa's dad had sent her here for weeks, alone. Luckily for me

Sofia turned out to be a great person. But how could Willa's dad have known that?

"I didn't," Sofia corrected me, though. "For many years I didn't know him at all. But now … now I feel like I do. Family is important to me, I hope you've seen that. But you might not realize how much it matters to my husband too. Mattias and I … we can't have children of our own, sadly. But we always knew we wanted to fill this house with family. Mattias says it's because of my good-Samaritan problem that we chose to foster instead of adopt. But really, it was because of him."

"Because of Mattias?"

"He didn't have a lot of family growing up. He was passed from foster home to foster home, never staying anywhere very long. He wanted to give kids like him the chance to grow up the way *he* would have wanted to. With animals and land and good food and love."

I chewed thoughtfully. Luca and Rosa and Antonio had got lucky, coming here.

"Anyway, I tell you this because it was Mattias who suggested that I reach out to your dad too." Sofia smiled softly. "A number of years ago, just after we were married, he asked why I didn't just send him an email. My parents had passed away and Scott was the only family I had left. So I wrote to him. I sent photos from the wedding, pictures of the farm, talked about life here … and then I waited to see if he wanted to write back."

"And he did?" Did Willa know all this? I doubted it.

"Not straight away. But after a month or so, I got an email back, with a family photo – very out-of-date now, of course," she added, looking me over. I stiffened, my heart starting to race as I imagined Sofia studying that photo and comparing it to me. I could only hope she didn't notice the all-too-obvious differences between the girl in that photo and me.

If she had, she didn't say anything, though. It was lucky for Willa and me that we were at an age where we were expected to change quickly.

"After that, we exchanged emails a couple of times a year. Until last Christmas, when suddenly Scott's messages became more frequent. He stopped sending photos, but he asked a lot of questions about our father instead. What it had been like growing up with him, how he'd been when he got older, how he'd died. If he'd been happy." Sofia gave me a sad smile. "I realized later, he was trying to decide what to do about his marriage. When he left your mum…

That's when it all made sense."

"He'd been so angry with his dad for leaving his family when he was younger," I said slowly, remembering what Willa had said in her dossier. "And now he was trying to decide whether to do the same thing to me and Mum."

"Exactly," Sofia said. "Anyway, when he wrote and asked if you could stay for a few weeks… I was so happy. It meant that those bridges were finally mended." She wrapped an arm round my shoulder and hugged me tight. I tried to smile, but really, I was worrying about all those messages Sofia and Willa's dad had exchanged – probably still were exchanging. Luca had already mentioned things that they knew about me – or about Willa – from her dad. How much else had he told them? I really had to concentrate on being Willa. What if I tripped up on a fact they knew and I didn't?

Sofia was oblivious to my churning stomach, though. "And now you're here, I'm even happier, because I get to know my wonderful niece."

Her words sparked the guilt in my chest again. Sofia had been nothing but kind, had answered all my questions honestly – and I was lying to her, every moment I stayed there.

But what else could I do? If I told the truth now, Willa would get into trouble too – and I'd have to go to London with Mabel, who would know the lengths I'd gone to just to avoid spending the summer with her.

There was nothing for it but to carry out the plan and meet Willa back at Heathrow in three weeks.

Until then...

"I'm happy to be here too, Aunt Sofia." I pulled the stack of recipe cards towards me. "Now, which of these are we making next?"

WILLA

The Westfield shopping centre was big, but not as huge as some of the malls I'd been to in America. I grabbed a map from a stand at the entrance, and scanned the list of shops.

"I think there's a good bookshop in here somewhere too," Mabel said, peering over my shoulder.

I was about to laugh and make a sarcastic remark, then remembered that Alice wouldn't find her comment hilarious. But honestly, who went to a shopping centre for books? Oh, right – Alice and Mabel. Urgh, I was probably going to have to spend some of my precious shopping day in the actual bookshop, just to keep up the Alice act.

I'd pestered Mabel about the budget on the Tube there, and it turned out that Alice's dad must be feeling *really* guilty about sending her home from Australia. It wasn't enough to go designer or anything, but enough to make a good dent in H&M's racks, and still leave me plenty to buy some bras that didn't dig into my ribs.

As I browsed through the shops, Mabel checking email on her phone behind me, I reminded myself that in three weeks, when I met Alice at Heathrow, we'd be swapping cases again and this whole clothes haul would be hers. That helped, somehow, with choosing which things to try on. I wasn't picking clothes for *me*, I was assembling a costume wardrobe for playing Alice.

I needed clothes that weren't *too* far from what Alice would normally wear, but just less … terrible. Things that Alice might wear if she was actually aware of fashion. Which, with some nudging from me, she could be.

Really, I might be the best thing that ever happened to Alice Wright.

Eventually, I settled on a few new outfits, plus bras and shoes. Sticking with Alice's 'jeans and T-shirt' look, I went with skinny jeans, a few cute tops (that had no sea-life related puns on them), and then went wild with the accessories to make things more fun. I agonized over an H&M dupe of a designer bag I'd been eyeing up in LA, but eventually had to admit that there was no way Alice would *ever* have carried it, so I left it on the shelf.

Still, the jewellery, sparkly flip-flops, and fun bag

I *did* buy would help make the outfits feel a little more like me. And the slightly more on-trend trainers I bought fitted better too. All in all, I was declaring the trip a success.

I tried to pretend I hadn't spotted the look of utter relief that it was over on Mabel's face as she paid. I felt kind of bad for her – she obviously wasn't a shopping person (which I totally could have told you from her wardrobe) but she'd followed me around all morning, made the right noises when I tried things on – with only one comment about my 'evolving style' – and hadn't complained once.

"Do you fancy the bookshop next?" I asked, trying to make it sound like the sort of thing I said every day.

Mabel's face lit up. "Great plan! Then we can get a late lunch in the food court before we head back."

It was a *very* late lunch by the time Mabel had finished in the bookshop. We ate street food from one of the stalls in the food court, while Mabel explained (in detail) about each of the four books she'd bought, and I pretended that I'd already read all the best books from the YA section, so hadn't chosen anything new.

Maybe I should start carrying a book around with me, like a prop. Something to make me look more

Alice. The last thing I wanted was Mabel telling Alice's dad that she was worried I was depressed because I'd lost interest in books, or something.

Alice's dad was loads more invested in his daughter's trip to London than my own parents were in my Italian Hell. There'd been a text message from Dad to make sure I'd got there safely, and a quick call from Mum to check it wasn't actually as dire as the message I'd sent her made out – which I'd taken huddled in my room with a duvet over my head to muffle my words. Other than that, I'd barely heard from my parents since I arrived in London. Well, apart from updates to their social-media channels, and a few photos of Edinburgh castle and the LA set at 5 a.m. for an early morning call, respectively.

Work was far more interesting than whatever I was doing, as usual.

Alice's dad, on the other hand, wasn't letting being in the middle of the stupid ocean keep him from checking up on his daughter – and having soppy late night calls with his girlfriend.

After the first time he called, my first night in London, Alice and I had come up with a warning system. OK, Alice had come up with it.

"Given the time difference, plus the work on the

boat, he's pretty much got to call at set times. And I know my dad, he's a creature of habit. Tonight he called me first, then you heard him call Mabel, right?" Alice hadn't waited for me to agree before she carried on talking. "I bet you he does the same every other night for the rest of the summer. Should be pretty easy for you to avoid having to speak to him when he's on the phone to her, since he'll already have spoken to *me*. Just make sure you're in your room or something around the time he always calls me, in case he mentions having spoken to you to Mabel, and we should be fine."

I was just glad Alice's dad was out of range for video calls. Those would have been pretty hard to explain.

After lunch, we caught the Tube back to Mabel's flat. She had to work at home that afternoon – something she sounded masses more guilty about than was really necessary. I told her I'd be fine, and planned to go exploring the neighbourhood around the flat some more.

But as we exited the Tube station nearest Mabel's flat, I spotted a newly familiar face.

"Hal!" I called, waving my arm above my head when he turned and looked around.

Beside me, Mabel frowned at her phone again.

I was guessing work. I hadn't really taken in *everything* she'd been talking about over lunch (I'd been mentally compiling outfits that I could make from the new pieces we'd bought, and how they'd look on a) me and b) Alice) but it seemed some research project she was working on was having money issues, and whoever was *supposed* to be solving it was clearly rubbish. Which explained all the panicky emails they kept sending her.

Well, if Mabel was about to announce she had to head back to the university for yet another meeting, then I was going to need entertaining. Plus Hal and I were due a discussion about how he could best act as my alibi while I went to my theatre course.

All my plans were coming together nicely, just as I'd known they would.

ALICE

HELP!

WILLA

What? What happened? Do I need to get packing and disappear before the police show up and arrest me for travelling on someone else's passport?

ALICE

Oh God, do you think that might happen? I thought once we were through passport control we were safe... How many laws do you think we've broken already?

WILLA

Alice. Calm down, it was a joke. We're under sixteen anyway, so they'd probably just blame our parents.

ALICE

THAT'S EVEN WORSE!

WILLA

So, why were you texting during the day if it's not an ACTUAL emergency? I thought we were catching up tonight?

ALICE

That's the emergency. There's some food festival in the village this week and it starts with a big party tomorrow night. Everyone's going and Antonio said he'd show me around...

WILLA

Antonio? Seventeen-year-old, six foot of Italian hotness, Antonio?

ALICE

That's the one.

WILLA

I'm really not seeing a problem here.

ALICE

Then you're not looking hard enough. I was all excited for maybe half an hour before the terrible reality set in.

ALICE

What was I thinking, saying yes? I mean, it's probably not a date anyway. But if it is ... what was I thinking? I can't go on a date!

ALICE

I mean, I've already written a list of at least ten major things that might go wrong.

WILLA

WILLA

Of course you have. So, what do you want me to do about them?

ALICE

Tell me what happens on a date. Tell me what to expect.

ALICE

And most of all

ALICE

TELL ME WHAT TO WEAR!

WILLA

Ha! That I can do. Actually, I just bought you basically a whole new wardrobe that you are going to LOVE.

ALICE

Except that wardrobe is in London. And I'm in Italy.

WILLA

Which is even better, because it means you have MY wardrobe.

ALICE

I don't understand your wardrobe.

WILLA

What's not to understand?

ALICE

How do I put them together? I mean, what do I wear with what? I'm not used to your style of clothes!

WILLA

Trust me, I know. I've seen your suitcase.

WILLA

Wait, what have you been wearing for the last week, then?

ALICE

Stuff I could make sense of. Like jeans and tops.

WILLA

So basically, the closest you could get to your own clothes.

ALICE

Yeah. I tried your flouncy skirt and red top but... Well, it went wrong and we're not talking about it.

WILLA

My wardrobe is wasted on you.

WILLA

But because I like you – and because you're being me right now – I will help you.

ALICE

Thank you! So, what do I wear to impress a boy?

WILLA

This really is new territory for you, isn't it?

ALICE

Totally.

WILLA

OK, let's start with something easy. Go find the denim skirt I packed – the one with the frayed hem, not the one with the patches. It's shorter.

WILLA

And once we've got the clothes sorted, you're going to have to video call so I can help you with your make-up and hair.

WILLA

And then we're going to talk about me for a while, because you're not the only one who's had new experiences this week, you know.

WILLA

OK?

WILLA

Alice?

ALICE

When you said shorter, you really weren't kidding, were you?

ALICE

It was hard to carry a basket full of cakes *and* tug down the edge of my skirt at the same time, but so far I was managing it. Willa's idea of acceptable village-food-festival wear was kind of different to mine, but I'd asked for her advice, so I had to take it. Which was why I was wearing the very short denim skirt with the frayed hem, and a bright red top that hung off my shoulders.

"Tuck it in," Willa had said, watching me through the laptop screen. "Now untuck half of it. No, not like that. Like this." Even with her demonstrating with her own top on the webcam, mine still didn't look quite like hers. She had sighed. "It'll do. Now, hair. Then make-up."

I'd attempted the Dutch plait she'd done in my hair on the plane three times before giving up. "OK, part it on the side, and spritz some of the stuff in the gold-and-pink bottle through it," Willa had instructed eventually. I'd done as I was told, my arms aching from holding them above my head, trying to braid my hair. "Now run your fingers through it and scrunch it up a bit. Perfect!"

Pausing to look in the mirror, I'd been amazed to see soft waves falling around my shoulders. My hair *never* did that. It felt like magic. And lots easier than Dutch braids.

"Make-up next!" Willa had announced, looking gleeful.

I'd drawn the line at the brow kit and the contouring, but even so I was wearing a lot more make-up than I was used to. Thick black mascara, a lip-gloss that matched my top, and even a touch of eyeliner. I'd assured Willa that, given my tendency to turn bright red at the slightest hint of embarrassment, blusher was *really* not needed.

The finished result made me look more like Willa – and less like myself – than ever before. I just hoped I could keep the Willa confidence that came with it for the whole night at the festival.

Even if Luca was looking between me and Antonio then rolling his eyes a lot.

"Are you dressing up for my brother?" Luca asked, as we walked together up the hill towards the village. "Or hoping to catch the eye of some other Italian guys at the festival?"

My eyes widened and I glanced quickly at Antonio to see if he'd heard. Given he was only a few steps ahead, talking with Mattias, I had to assume he did, although he gave no sign. I swallowed down the embarrassed panic rising in me, and focused on staying Willa – she wouldn't be thrown by a comment like that, so neither would I.

"Neither," I said, as airily as I could. The effect was only slightly ruined by the wobble in my voice.

I was a different person here in Italy – not just because I was pretending to be Willa, but because all the things that made me Alice had been taken away. I wasn't a professor's brainy daughter, named 'most likely to die locked in a library' by my classmates. I wasn't the one who never went to parties, or who hated clothes shopping. And most of all, I wasn't the girl whose mum had died.

I was someone new, which was kind of scary and brilliant at the same time.

And tonight, I wanted to be the sort of girl who'd go to a festival in a remote Italian town on a hill and not worry about how she didn't speak the language well enough yet, or overthink what would happen if someone tried to talk to her, or panic about somehow saying something embarrassing or rude in her learner

Italian. I didn't want to be the Alice who'd need to plan every moment of the evening, or know exactly what happened next. I wanted to be the girl who'd smile and laugh and love every second of it. A spontaneous, free Alice. An Alice who'd just enjoy herself without getting anxious or shy or awkward.

I wanted to be the sort of girl that Antonio – or any boy, really – would enjoy spending time with. Who'd get asked to a party because a guy wanted to go with her – not because he was just being kind to his foster mother's niece. (My latest theory was that Sofia had asked him to look after me at the festival.)

I'd spent most of the last twenty-four hours imagining how Antonio might hold my hand as we walked around the stalls, or lean in close to explain what they were selling, his mouth against my ear so I could hear him better over the party going on around us. Imagined him not caring about the festival at all himself, just wanting to watch me enjoy it.

I'd even imagined that he would kiss me.

Not that I was *ever* going to admit that to Luca.

I knew that Antonio probably didn't think about me that way at all. But that could change, right? If I let go, if I laughed and danced and had fun in a way that I'd never managed as Alice – maybe Antonio would start to see me differently. Or at the very least forget about the socks in my bra thing.

"People really go all out for the festival," Luca said, and I was grateful he'd changed the subject. "Last year there was dancing and music until one in the morning. And the cakes..." He shook his head. "I'd never tasted anything like it."

We heard the music first, when we were barely more than halfway up the hill. Guitars, drums and other instruments I couldn't identify by sound alone. It was early evening, the sun still hovering in the sky, lowering itself slowly towards the stone walls of the village, turning them red and gold and orange.

Rosa let out a little whoop of excitement, turning cartwheels on the grass beside the path while Antonio held her basket as well as his own. Luca's grin was wider than I'd ever seen it, a flash of white teeth against his tanned skin as he smiled at me.

I couldn't help it. I could feel the anticipation jangling through me like bells on a string, all ringing at once.

"Ready, Willa?" Antonio asked, offering me his hand with a smile.

"As I'll ever be." I took a deep breath, then reached out to hold his hand, trying not to blush at the feel of his skin under my fingertips. He couldn't see my heart, so I let that beat double time with excitement.

Rosa skipped through the gate first, followed by Luca, then Antonio and me. Together, we stepped through the ancient stone archway into the main piazza – and then I stopped, almost instantly.

I hadn't been prepared for this. It was *nothing* like the summer fete I'd thought it would be.

Heat from the many cooking stalls hit my face, while the music and singing rang through my head. Flags and decorations hung from every balcony, every stone cornice, in every colour imaginable. And in the centre of the piazza, people were dancing – brightly coloured skirts flaring and black boots hitting stone.

But most of all I heard laughter and I saw smiles. The whole community, happy to be together, celebrating their village and their history through their love of food, music and dance.

Suddenly, what clothes I chose to wear to this celebration seemed like the least important thing in the world.

"Shall we catch up with the others?" Antonio asked, sounding amused. When I looked up at him, unable to reply except by blinking, he smiled. "It can be a bit overwhelming the first time you see a festival like this. You don't have these at home?"

"Not like this," I said. "Well, not that I've ever been to, anyway." Maybe other people spent their weekends at parties like this, while I was hiding away in my room with a book. Maybe this was what I'd been missing all along.

Not any more, though.

Antonio and I caught up with Luca and Rosa, which, although I'd sort of hoped Antonio and I would be alone, was nice too. Sofia and Mattias had already distributed the dishes that we'd spent the last couple of days preparing to the appropriate tables, and were now sitting with friends in the centre of the piazza sharing a carafe of wine. We waved as we passed and wove through the crowds, sampling the food at every stall, pausing to listen to the music as we reached the end of the piazza where the band were performing.

A stream of dancers swooped past us, twirling and twisting, the women's arms raised above their heads as they swayed and moved. They were so beautiful, with their skirts flying loose in the breeze.

I'm not a dancer. My parents gave up on my ballet classes after Grade One because I was always looking at my feet and chewing my hair. Well, that and the fact that I have no natural rhythm. But even *my* hips started to sway to the heavy beat as the music filled me.

I was focused so completely on the music, my eyes half closed to feel it better, that I didn't see the dancer who swung out of formation until she reached out to grab my hands. My eyes flew wide open as I was pulled into the dance, and I saw that Rosa was beside me with another dancer. Rosa was spinning and singing at the top of her voice, her head thrown back with happiness.

I wanted that too. That joy. Not caring what she looked like, or who was watching, or if she was making a fool of herself.

The dancers had dragged in all sorts of bystanders to join in their performance, and none of them seemed to have any more idea what to do than I did. But it didn't matter. Clinging to my partner's hands, I let her twirl me around, spinning me off until another dancer caught me, and the whole move started again. I spun around the piazza, laughing so hard I could hardly breathe.

I caught Luca's eye as I danced past the spot where we'd stood to watch. He was clapping along in time to the music, one foot stamping on the ground too. He grinned at me as I spun around again, falling into the arms of one of the other dancers just as the music came to a triumphant halt.

Breathing hard, I disentangled myself from the dance troupe and headed back to the sidelines before the music started up again. I needed a minute to recover if I was going to dance any more! Rosa, on the other hand, was still dancing, even though there was no music. And Antonio...

"Where's Antonio?" I asked Luca, glancing around the piazza to look for him.

"Oh, he met a ... friend," Luca replied. But he didn't meet my eye as he said it.

And then I knew why.

Antonio hadn't gone far – just into a little alleyway behind the stall nearest to us. Where he was kissing a beautiful, dark-haired dancer from the troupe.

Of course.

My whole body felt too hot, and my chest was tight. I couldn't look back at Luca, couldn't bear to see him laughing at me. Stupid little Alice who'd let herself hope, even just for a moment, that Antonio might actually have noticed *her*.

I'd known. I'd told myself over and over that this wasn't a date.

But it seemed my crush-ridden heart hadn't quite believed me. Until now.

WILLA

Obviously it was Hal who put the first obstacle in my path.

"I *can't* spend my summer just being your alibi, Willa."

"Alice," I corrected, glancing around us. Fortunately, no one else in the park by Mabel's flat seemed to be paying attention to two teenagers sitting on the grass in the shade of some big old tree. "And why not?"

"Um, because I actually have my own life?"

I tried not to look too surprised at that revelation. "So, what will you be doing when you're not being my alibi?" I mean, I didn't want to interrupt his important computer-game-playing time, or whatever it was boys like Hal did over summer. That would be *terrible*.

Hal looked away, obviously embarrassed. I knew it. He didn't *actually* have any plans.

But then he said, "I got accepted to this great science camp for the summer. It's every afternoon next week, at Queen Anne University's other campus site, across town."

"Where, exactly?" A new plan was already formulating in my brain.

Hal pulled out his phone and opened the maps app, bringing up the location with a few swipes of his finger. Taking the phone from him, I smiled as I enlarged the map just enough to show the theatre where my course was held. It couldn't be more than a five- or ten-minute walk between the two.

"Perfect," I said.

Hal grabbed his phone back, his forehead crumpled in confusion. "Why do I already know I won't like whatever idea you're about to come up with?"

In fairness to him, Hal had grasped how being friends with me worked in a very short time. Smart guy.

Still, I flashed him my most innocent smile in the hope it would encourage him to play along a bit longer.

"I'm registered on a theatre course just around the corner, three afternoons a week for the next two weeks."

"You are, or Alice is?" Hal asked.

"Me, myself, personally." I rolled my eyes. It wasn't really *that* confusing. And why would *Alice* be going on a theatre course?

"OK, so?"

Leaning forwards, with my elbows on my knees, I made sure I had Hal's full attention before I shared the plan. "So, we tell Mabel that I'm going to science camp with you next week, but actually I slip off and go to my course instead."

"That ... could work, I suppose," Hal admitted. "Except, my camp is only one week. What do we do in week two?"

I shrugged. "We'll figure it out."

That made him fidget nervously with the strap of his backpack. I got the feeling that Hal was a planner, like Alice.

"Remind me why I'm helping you again?" he asked.

"Because Alice will be really, really grateful," I said. Which wasn't *exactly* a lie – Alice would be grateful he hadn't dobbed us in, at least.

"You've told her you're hanging out with me?"

"Of course!"

"What did she say?" Hal sounded eager now, far more so than he had at the idea of hanging out with *me* for the summer.

I tried to find a way to put Alice's comments that would convince him to keep helping us. Telling him that she'd actually said, *You and Hal, together for the*

166

summer? That should be … interesting, probably wasn't it.

"To tell you thank you, and that she's really looking forward to seeing you again soon." I jumped to my feet, reaching down a hand to pull Hal up too. He groaned, but followed all the same. "Now, come on, let's go and find Mabel and ask her about science camp."

As I'd expected, Mabel was *thrilled* by the plan. I mean, she had a lot of questions (which I let Hal answer) and we had to hammer out exactly how everything would work – how we'd get there and back, where we'd meet etc. But overall, she was definitely in favour. I got the feeling she was going to be doing a lot more work than she'd planned during my visit, and this way she didn't have to worry about entertaining me 24/7 as well. Of course, it helped that science camp was absolutely the sort of thing that Alice would sign up for.

"Oh, your dad will be so pleased for you!" Mabel said excitedly. "You'll text him and let him know? I know he'll want to call and talk to you about it, as soon as he can."

"Absolutely," I agreed, mentally making a note to

text Alice and warn her that she needed to tell her dad the good news. I might not mention the Hal part just yet, though.

The important thing was, I started my course at the Old Row Theatre on Monday – and by the end of the summer, I'd have a job on *Heatherside*, and my dad back in my life full time. Everything would be perfect.

ALICE

I didn't mean to run away from the others, exactly. And I definitely didn't want them to know that I was upset at seeing Antonio kissing some other girl. But I knew what the tightening of my chest meant, the way I was struggling to catch my breath.

When Mum died, I started getting panic attacks a couple of times a week. Then, it tended to be when I realized I was all alone, and I didn't know what to do next. As time went on, I learned to manage them better, until I sometimes went whole months without one. And even when they did happen, I knew what to do.

These days, they came when there was too much in my head. When all my thoughts crashed and swirled around my brain, too fast for me to even make sense of them. Like now.

Idiot! Why on earth did you think Antonio could ever be interested it you? You thought wearing a short skirt would change anything? Everyone will be laughing at you now. They've probably been laughing at you all along. Willa would never have got herself into this position. They're bound to figure out you're not her any minute now and send you to London. And what are the chances Mabel will want you after this...

I sucked in the deepest breath I could manage. I was catastrophizing. Nothing had really happened. Nobody had died.

The world keeps turning, Alice. There's always another, better day ahead. My mum's voice, again.

I blinked away the tears and took another deep breath. My heart was starting to slow to something approaching normal speed again, at last, and my chest didn't feel like it was being crushed by the tide against the rocks.

It was a start. Now I just needed a few minutes to get myself together. To get back to Alice, instead of the Willa-wannabe I'd tried to be that evening. Whatever everyone else believed, I really *wasn't* Willa, and some new clothes couldn't change that.

Luca found me, tucked away on a set of steps that led to the closed bank on the edge of the piazza. I tensed, waiting for the inevitable teasing.

But the laughter never came.

"You OK?" Luca settled on to the step beside me, leaving a few inches between us.

"I'm fine," I lied. "Just got a bit claustrophobic with all the people. Needed some air."

"So you hid away in a dark corner with walls on three sides and a stall just in front. Makes total sense."

I didn't have a response to that.

"Is it my brother?" he asked.

"It's not Antonio, I promise."

"Right." He didn't believe me, obviously.

"Really. It's not like I thought I was here with him on a date or anything."

"Which is why you dressed up and held his hand." There was a simmering anger under Luca's words that I instinctively read as being directed at me. Then I saw the glare he sent across the piazza, to where I'd last seen Antonio and realized the truth. He was angry with his brother.

"Dressing up wasn't for him," I explained. "Not really. Yes, it was nice to be asked but I knew he meant it in a friendly way. In fact, I figured Sofia probably asked him to ask me."

Luca shook his head. "She wouldn't do that. But she probably asked him to make you feel included. And Antonio doesn't know how to talk to girls if he isn't flirting."

I smiled. "The point is, I knew this wasn't a date or

anything." I had to keep reminding myself of that. My hopes were not Antonio's fault.

"But you were upset when you saw him kissing Maria."

So that was her name. "Is she his girlfriend?"

"I don't think so." Luca shrugged. "Just a girl he knows from school. But it's hard to tell with Antonio."

He sat up, straightening his legs out in front of him as he leaned back on his hands. "So, if it wasn't for him, what's the reason for the outfit?"

I blushed a little as I tugged down the end of Willa's denim skirt again. "A friend of mine... Alice. She keeps telling me I should dress up a bit more. When I mentioned the festival, she insisted on picking my outfit for me. This is what she chose."

I looked away, focusing on the toes of my canvas trainers. "I was trying to be someone else, I guess. More like her."

And for a moment, when I'd been dancing, I'd felt like a different person altogether. Not Alice, but not Willa either. Just free, I guess.

Now I was back to being Alice-pretending-to-be-Willa, and suddenly it all felt too much.

My throat got tight and I could feel the hot rush of tears behind my eyes. I wouldn't cry in front of Luca, though. I wouldn't. I wouldn't…

"Are you crying?"

"No." Definite lie. "Maybe."

Tentatively, Luca put his arm round my shoulder, so lightly I could barely feel it resting there. "I'm sorry my brother's an idiot."

A burst of soggy laughter flew from my mouth. "It's not Antonio. I just … sometimes I think I should never have come to Italy at all."

If I hadn't swapped places with Willa, I wouldn't be lying to all these people I liked, and trying to be something I wasn't.

Luca patted my shoulder awkwardly, which just made me sob again.

"My mum used to say, sometimes, when I was sad, that I should think of a time or a place where I was happy instead, and imagine I was back there." It was the first time he'd mentioned his mother. "You could try it, maybe?"

I nodded, and closed my eyes, searching for a happier thought, a happier time.

Which led me back to my own mum, naturally, telling me the tale of a waterfall that could wash away all your worries.

I'd planned on telling Antonio about that waterfall

tonight. Asking him if he'd help me find it, even.

"You're frowning," Luca pointed out. "Happy thoughts aren't supposed to make you frown. You're doing it wrong."

I opened my eyes. "I'm not. I was just thinking about my mum. She told me about a waterfall somewhere in Italy. One she always wanted to go to. It's called..." I tried to drag up the name from my memory, forcing my mouth to make the unfamiliar Italian words. "Cascada del Fuga?"

"Cascata della Fuga," Luca corrected me. "Yeah, it's not too far from here."

I sat bolt upright, my tears and Antonio forgotten. "Really?" I'd tried to look, once or twice, but I hadn't got very far. The only sites I'd found were in Italian, and the translation features were worse than useless.

"Well, not that close, either. Hang on." He took his phone out of his pocket, and pulled up one of the websites that had baffled me. "It's about two and a half hours away," he said, after scrolling through a few pages. "It might take a few buses and a bit of walking, but we could get there. If you wanted to see it, I mean."

I looked up at him. "We?"

He shrugged. "I figure you'd probably get lost on

your own. I mean, if it's not ordering gelato, your Italian is still a work in progress."

"True." I tried to imagine Antonio offering to take me two and half hours to visit a waterfall, just because I'd mentioned I'd like to see it, and failed. "If you wouldn't mind…" I gave him a shy smile. "I really would love to go. It would mean a lot." Excitement bubbled up inside me at the idea of actually seeing Mum's waterfall, at last.

Luca beamed. "Good! Then we'll start planning. I'll need to look up the bus routes…"

"Tomorrow," I said, as he turned back to his phone. "Right now, I want to see if there are any of Sofia's lemon cakes left."

"I doubt it." Luca slipped his phone back in his pocket, looking relieved that my crying was over. So was I, to be honest. "They're the best thing here."

"Let's check anyway."

But as we crossed the piazza to the stall that had the lemon cakes, I wasn't thinking about food at all.

I was thinking about a waterfall that could wash away every worry, and every single panic attack.

WILLA

Monday morning I was fizzing with excitement. I chose my outfit with care – skinny jeans, and one of Alice's hilarious T-shirts over a crop top I'd bought on my shopping trip. (Obviously the T-shirt was getting shoved in my bag the moment Mabel was out of sight.) I'd also made good use of the make-up I'd bought when we were shopping. I'd stuck with a fairly neutral, believable Alice look for now, but I had a full stash of stuff with me for taking it up a notch before I got to the theatre.

At the theatre, I'd be Willa again, not Alice. Full-on, real me, Willa.

I couldn't wait.

Mabel looked amused as she walked me to the Tube to meet Hal. "I don't think I've ever seen anyone quite so excited about science camp," she said. "And I was the quintessential science nerd in school."

I shrugged, and tried to look a little more nonchalant. "It's just nice to be doing something productive with my summer," I said virtuously, in my best Alice voice.

Hal was already waiting for us by the entrance so, after going over the plan one last time for luck, Mabel waved us goodbye and we headed down into the Underground.

I snagged a seat on the first train that came along, and Hal sat down opposite me, looking nervous.

"It's going to be fine," I assured him, fishing in my bag for my brow kit. "I've got this whole thing worked out." For some reason, that just made him look more nervous.

I was totally right, though. We arrived at our stop in plenty of time, and I waved him into the Queen Anne campus before pulling off Alice's 'science camp' T-shirt, getting out my phone and double-checking the route to the Old Row Theatre.

Despite being early, I wasn't the first one there – in fact, I was one of the last. Seemed like everyone else was just as eager as me. As we all waited to check in with a girl with blue hair sitting at a table in the foyer, I eyed up the competition.

There was a group of four girls who looked a year or so older than me, all in almost-matching outfits, so I figured they were friends. There were two guys, but that was all. One lounged with confidence against the stair banister, checking his teeth in the selfie camera on his phone. The other was shorter and skinnier than me, with a shock of bright red hair – not ginger, actually dyed red – who was rifling through his satchel. Then there were another five individual girls, ranging in age from around thirteen to sixteen, all looking a little nervous – you know, eyes wide as they took in all the theatre posters, or picking at their nail varnish as they stared at their feet.

Nobody who'd be a problem, I decided.

Finally it was my turn to register. "Hi, I'm Willa Martyn," I said, handing over my registration paperwork. The name felt even stranger to say than it normally would. I'd almost got used to being Alice over the last few days. But I'd never been Willa Martyn. (If Mum and Dad got divorced and he disowned me totally, would I have to take Mum's maiden name? How did these things even work?) Mum was married by the time she got her big break, and everyone knew her as Sarra Andrews, not Sarra Martyn.

"Willa… Willa… Huh. It says here that your registration was cancelled?" The girl with the blue hair looked up at me, while still pointing at the big X next to my name on the list.

No. No, this could not be happening. Not after everything I'd gone through to get here.

Mum must have emailed or called them without telling me.

Well, I'd just have to talk my way out of this, the same way I'd talked my way in.

"Billie," I said, reading the name off her badge. "Trust me, there is no way I'd cancel on the opportunity to be here this summer! Look at my form. I registered for this course the day it opened for bookings. It's my dream to be here. In fact, I just flew in all the way from LA for it."

Billie frowned down at the list. "I guess it *could* be a mistake."

I nodded. Vigorously. "I think it must be."

"OK, well, we actually had a last-minute dropout this morning and I haven't called the first person on the waiting list yet, so there's still a space for you." My heart started to lift again. And then it dropped, like a rock, with her next words. "We'll just need to speak to your parent or guardian to confirm."

I'd never thought as quickly as I did in that moment, watching Billie reach for the phone.

"Billie," I said softly. "Do you know who my parents *are*? Trust me, they're a little too busy right now to deal with something this minor."

She looked sceptical, so I pulled out my phone and

opened up Mum's Twitter feed, scrolling down to the last photo of the two of us. Then I showed it to Billie.

Her eyes widened as she recognized me – and more importantly, Mum. "But it says here your name is Martyn, not Andrews."

"Mum's maiden name," I explained with a little shrug. "I wanted to get here on my own merits, not my parents' names. But now I'm here... I mean, I could call Mum but she's filming in LA and the schedule is crazy, and Dad's on stage in Edinburgh this afternoon, so..."

"Right, sure." Billie quickly printed me an extra name tag and handed it over. "I'm sure it'll be fine."

I gave her my widest smile. "I really appreciate it, thanks. Any time I can do anything for you." By which I meant, if my *parents* could do anything, and she knew it.

No way she was dobbing me in now.

"Enjoy the camp," Billie said, looking a lot happier about the world.

"Oh, I will." I took my badge, pinned it to my jeans pocket rather than ruin my top, and stepped away from the desk.

Suddenly, a large and imposing figure appeared at the top of the stairs, wearing a bright orange velvet

jacket over a flouncy white shirt. Vincent Paloma –
our director for the week.

"Ah, my budding thespians. Are we all here, Billie?
No, I can spot a couple of notable exceptions already."

I looked around, towards the door. We were missing
people? People he already knew?

"I'm sure they'll be with us shortly," Mr Paloma
went on. "Now, if you will all follow me, we shall
begin your introduction to *the stage.*"

Vincent Paloma ("Call me Vincent," he told us) was
a national star of stage and screen – according to his
autobiography, which I'd read excerpts of online.
He'd starred in BBC dramas, Shakespeare on the
stage, radio plays, arty films (mostly twenty years or
more ago) and, recently, a lot of pantomime. Mum
said he used to have talent, but now he mostly stuck
to teaching. I hadn't been entirely sure what she
meant by that at the time, but I was getting a better
idea now I'd met him.

The important thing was, he knew the business. He
had contacts, he had history, and he had the casting
director from *Heatherside* coming in two weeks to watch

us perform. So really, it didn't much matter if he seemed more impressed with himself than I was.

At least, that's what I told myself.

We all took a seat in the audience of the small Old Row Theatre auditorium, while Vincent paced across the stage giving us his welcome speech (mostly a recap of the most exciting bits from the autobiography, as far as I could tell).

Then he stopped pacing, stood dead centre of the stage, and stared out at us. Suddenly the lights went out, and a single spotlight illuminated his face. Looking up at the back of the theatre, I could see Billie's blue hair shining through the window of the lighting box as she worked the spot.

"Most of all, you are here to learn from me. I will make it my mission to convey to you all you need to know to forge a career in this fickle, faithless but fabulous business we call simply, the Show."

We sat in silence, still staring at him, until clapping sounded from the side of the stage (the wings, I reminded myself). Belatedly, we all joined in, as a beautiful redheaded girl, not much older than me, walked on to the stage, followed by two other girls, both equally gorgeous.

"Well said, Uncle Vinnie," the redhead said,

throwing her arms round Vincent. "I'm sure we all know just how *privileged* we are to be here. These are the friends I was telling you about," she said, motioning to the other girls. "They can join us, right?"

"Of course! Anything for my favourite goddaughter."

"While the rest of us had to audition twice, fill in endless paperwork *and* pay for the privilege," the girl next to me – Daisy, according to her name tag – muttered. I nodded in agreement, even as Vincent motioned his goddaughter and her friends to join us in the audience.

"Now," he said, clapping his hands together as the lights came back up. "We're going to start with some warm-ups. Everyone up on the stage, please!"

By the time my first afternoon at the theatre was over, I'd learned three things.

1. I hate doing trust falls.

2. Vincent's goddaughter, Tuppence, already went to the best stage school in London, as did her friends, so I had no idea why they had to intrude on *my* summer camp.

3. If it wasn't for the *Heatherside* casting director

watching us at the end of our second week, I'd be wondering if this course was worth all the bother.

That last was only increased by the discovery of Hal, sitting hunched up against the wall outside the stage door when I left at six o'clock.

"What are you doing here? I thought I was going to meet you at the station?" I ignored the sniggers behind me as Tuppence and her friends exited the theatre.

"Is she talking to a *homeless person*?" I heard one of them say, with exaggerated amazement.

Hal stood up before any of them could offer him fifty pence for a cup of tea.

"We *were* meeting at the station," he said. "But that was before I realized that my course finishes a whole hour before yours."

"You couldn't just hang out at the university?"

"I did!" Hal was getting agitated now. Probably not a good sign. "But then it turned out that *Mabel was visiting the other campus today*!"

"What! What was she doing there? What happened?" If Mabel realized I'd lied about attending science camp, all bets were off – and I wasn't sure how good a liar Hal was without me there to back him up. What if he'd given the game away already?

"I don't know what she was doing there, because I hid, of course!"

My heartbeat gradually returned to the medically recommended tempo. "So she didn't even see you? Way to give a girl a heart attack." Swinging my bag up on to my shoulder, I started walking towards the Tube.

"She didn't see me *this time*," Hal corrected, as he chased behind me. "What if she swings by the campus another day? Or every day? I can't keep jumping into the girls' loos to avoid her."

"You ran into the girls' loos? What if that's where *she* was going?"

"I didn't think about that at the time," Hal admitted. "But what if she stops by the science camp and you're not there?"

"You brazen it out," I said, with a shrug.

"I do what?"

"You *lie*, Hal. Tell her I'm running an errand for the teacher, or I've nipped to the loo, or whatever."

Hal didn't look entirely comfortable with the idea. "What if she decides to hang around to see you?"

"I don't think she will," I said, thinking it through. "She was all 'this is your big adventure in the city' when I told her about it. She won't want to hover."

"But if she does?" Hal pressed.

"Then you'll just have to cover for me somehow." He didn't look too pleased about that prospect either. "For Alice, of course," I added, to remind him why he was doing this.

Hal sighed. "So what do I do for the hour after I finish? If Mabel is meeting you at the Tube every afternoon, I need to be there with you, right? She knows my dad only lives around the corner. And I can't risk her seeing me hanging around at the university without you, once the camp is over. I'm not a good enough liar for that."

"Come to the theatre," I said on impulse. "You can hang out there and wait for me, then we'll head home together."

"They won't mind?"

To be honest, I had no idea. But I was sure we could figure something out. "It'll be fine. Now, more interestingly, what am *I* going to do while you're at the university tomorrow afternoon?" Tuesdays and Thursdays the theatre was used for a drama course for seven- to twelve-year-olds, while us older kids got it the other three days a week. "Because I'm *definitely* not hanging out at science camp."

WILLA

So? How did the date go?

ALICE

It wasn't a date.

ALICE

And we're adding it to the list of things we're never talking about again.

WILLA

That good, huh?

ALICE

Worse. How was the theatre course? Worth all the drama it took to get you there?

WILLA

Jury's still out.

WILLA

And Hal almost blew the whole thing with Mabel.

WILLA

Luckily I've fixed things now.

ALICE

I can't believe you roped Hal into acting as your alibi.

ALICE

How did you even manage that?

WILLA

I told you! His gigantic crush on you...

ALICE

I hope you're wrong about that.

ALICE

Crushes are the worst.

ALICE

It took a few days of planning, and staring at maps and bus routes on my laptop screen, to figure out exactly how we were going to get there. But with Luca's translation skills, we had all the information we needed. I saved one of the photos from the best website to my phone, and set it as my new background instead of the photo of Willa and her mum.

I might still be Willa to everyone in Italy, but I needed to go to the Cascata della Fuga as Alice, or else what was the point?

At night, I lay in bed remembering everything Mum had told me about the magical waterfall – which to be honest wasn't much, as she had never been there either. She'd only heard stories from friends who had been. But those stories were enough to keep the magic alive for me.

"Are we going to tell Sofia where we're going?" I asked Luca, as he wrote down bus times from the screen for us. "I mean, this trip is going to take us all day for definite."

Luca chewed on the end of his pencil as he considered. "We can tell her we're taking the bus to the next town from the village – Lunice," he said, after a moment. "It's a not a total lie, because we *will* be going there. We'll just be catching another bus afterwards. Anyway, I've done that journey before plenty of times, so she won't worry so much about that. Otherwise she might make Antonio go with us."

I pulled a face. I *definitely* didn't want that.

One good thing about my panic attack at the festival: seeing Antonio kissing Maria seemed to have crushed my crush for good. Since that night, it was as if I could see clearly again. See Antonio as just another boy – not someone so high above me and everyone else.

It was kind of a relief and kind of sad at the same time.

"OK, so we just take stuff as if we're going into Lunice. That's easy."

"You're going to want to wear trainers, though." Luca glanced down at my/Willa's flip-flops. "It's a proper walk at the other end."

"Don't worry about me." Willa might not be much of a hiker, but I'd explored more cliff paths and sea caves with my dad than Luca could imagine. "Just make sure we pack plenty of water."

"And snacks," Luca added. "Definitely snacks."

The first part of our journey was pretty uneventful.

We'd decided to take the trip on a Thursday – mostly because that was one of only two days when the buses we needed both ran, and partly because we knew that Sofia already had plans to take Rosa to a friend's house that day, so she couldn't beg to come along. As much as I liked Rosa, taking an eight year old hiking to a waterfall wasn't my idea of fun.

Luca and I walked up to the village and found the right bus stop without trouble. Luca had already managed to eat most of our snacks by the time the bus came, but I figured we could buy more when we stopped in Lunice to catch the next bus.

Lunice was a pretty town – at least, the parts I saw as we walked across the main piazza to the second bus stop. Then we were off out into the Italian countryside, watching for something to tell us when to get off.

"How will we know when it's our stop?" I asked Luca, but he had his head resting on his hoodie and his legs stretched out in the aisle, his eyes closed.

I elbowed him in the ribs.

"You need to worry less," he said, turning away from me and resettling his makeshift pillow. "This bus is basically only going one place. Someone will yell when it's time to get off."

"Are you sure?"

Luca looked back to roll his eyes at me, but he was smiling, which was a little more reassuring. "I said I'd get you to your waterfall and I will. So relax and enjoy the trip. OK?"

"OK."

"Good." Then he put ear buds in so he could ignore me completely.

I sat back and stared out of the window, fretting every time the bus slowed to a stop to let someone on or off.

In the end, though, Luca was right. The bus pulled up into a small village – much smaller than Tusello – and the driver called out something that clearly meant 'everybody off'.

Luca, who I'd thought was fast asleep, rolled to his feet in no time, and waited for me to gather up my book and journal so we could disembark.

"Where now?" I asked, as the bus roared off again, leaving us on the side of the road.

"Now we walk." He glanced down at my feet, spotting that I'd changed Willa's usual flip-flops for the pair of trainers I'd worn on the flight. "Good choice."

To start, the road out of the village was dry and dusty, the sun beating down on the back of my neck so hard that I insisted on stopping to reapply sun cream (Luca rolled his eyes).

We chatted as we walked – not about anything that mattered, but about little things. Luca told me stories about his life, but I noticed quickly that most of them happened after he came to stay with Sofia. And if they were from before, they were about school, or Rosa and Antonio. Nothing about his parents.

He asked questions too, about my life in the UK. I tried to think of the anecdotes from my life that sounded most Willa-ish, but there weren't many. So mostly I just listened, and thought about what was waiting for me at the waterfall.

After a while, the path swerved into the shade of a row of trees. Then the row grew wider and, before I knew it, we were deep in a wood. The sound of running water – fast flowing, crashing against the stones – grew louder as we walked, and I knew the waterfall couldn't be far.

Suddenly, my feet stopped moving. It wasn't a choice – my feet just sort of made the decision for me.

It took Luca a moment to notice. I'm sure it looked like I'd just turned into a statue, right there in the middle of the forest path.

But inside, everything was swirling. All I could hear in my head was my mum's voice – telling me stories, reciting her old sayings, singing as she cooked the dinner.

What if, by completing her bucket list for her, by asking the waterfall to get rid of my worries, I lost her for good?

I wanted to say goodbye to the anxiety and the fear but those were also the moments when I felt my mum's presence the most, heard her voice in my head.

"What's the matter?" Luca asked.

"I'm not sure I want to do this," I said.

Luca sighed and started walking back towards me. "You couldn't have figured this out two bus rides ago?" he said jokily.

"Sorry." I couldn't think of anything else to say.

"Willa. You wanted to come here. When we were

researching it, I could tell … this is important to you, right? I don't know why, but this waterfall matters."

I nodded stiffly. Luca dropped his rucksack and sat down on a fallen log. "So. What changed your mind? Was it the dark and scary woods? Or the rushing river?"

"Neither." I sat down next to him. I needed to find an excuse that fitted with Willa's story. "It's just … you know how sometimes you build something up in your mind and then when you finally see it or experience it, it's not as great as you imagined?"

Luca frowned in confusion. "Wait … the legend goes that the waterfall washes away worries. Are you … worried that the waterfall might not actually have magical powers after all?" His voice was only gently teasing, and I knew that he was genuinely trying to understand my freak-out. But he was wrong.

I was worried that it *would*. Which was ridiculous. *What's the worst thing that could happen?*

The worst was that I'd stop hearing my mum's voice in my head. Well, no, actually the worst thing was that I'd fall into the waterfall somehow and die. But even I had to admit that was unlikely.

A waterfall couldn't take my mum away from me. *Now, what's the best thing that could happen?*

I could let go of my worries, like Mum promised. I could feel free again, the way I had when I was dancing. I could move on with my life.

It was time to take the next step towards being the person I was meant to be – not the fearful Alice I had been since Mum's death, and not Willa either. Just me.

Is it worth the risk?

Yes.

Happiness is always worth the risk.

I got to my feet. "You're right. I'm being stupid."

"So we *are* going to see the waterfall?" Luca jumped up too, ready to follow me.

"Yes. We are going to see the probably-not-magical waterfall."

Because the real magic I needed was all me.

I was ready to say goodbye and move on.

WILLA

Tuesday, I spent the afternoon exploring Covent Garden and Leicester Square, while Hal went to science camp. Bored, I entertained myself taking photos of the London I was discovering, before remembering I couldn't post them to my Instagram account. What was the point of living the London life if I couldn't even share it online?

Frustrated, I added a filter to a shot of the cinema where all the movie premieres took place, without me in it, and loaded it to my account with the caption 'Throwback Tuesday. Wish I was in London again this summer. #imisslondon #italianhell'. I figured the only person who mattered that was likely to see it was my mum, and it wouldn't do any harm to remind her that I was still mad with her about how my summer turned out.

No need for her to know it hadn't worked out that way at all, just yet.

At the end of the afternoon I met Hal again to catch the Tube home. Mabel was waiting for me at the station.

"How was your day?" she asked, as we walked back towards her flat. Already it felt like our routine, like it was something we'd do every day, for months. "Learn anything interesting?"

"Um..." I tried to remember what Hal had said they'd been doing that day. I'd have to actually *listen* tomorrow. I'd got him to type the details into my phone yesterday to text to Alice, so she could update her dad accurately, but apparently I needed to know too. "A few things. Oh, but the funniest part was when Hal almost blew up the lab." *That* story I definitely remembered.

Wednesday, we spent all afternoon running short scenes and monologues in different styles, and different combinations of people, while Vincent and Billie observed and made notes on a clipboard. It was tons better than the trust falls and ice-breakers they'd had us doing on Monday – at least we got to actually *act* this time.

It was strange, pretending to be someone other than Alice now. I was so used to playing her part, to inhabiting her life, it was difficult to drop it to become Willa again, let alone a fictional character. But soon enough all my drama lessons from school came back to me, and I focused on thinking about who the character was and what they wanted, then trying to show that in my body and my voice.

Not that Vincent seemed to notice how hard I was trying, or how great I was. Mostly, he just praised Tuppence a lot. (Daisy said that her father was someone famous, which was why he made such a fuss about her. I made a mental note to 'accidentally' mention my parents in his hearing some time soon. But then I realized... Even though I didn't *think* Vincent was still in touch with my mum, what if he used this as an excuse to contact her? I couldn't risk it.)

The best part of the afternoon was when we got put into small groups – three actors and a director. Each group was given a short script to act out, with the director in charge of deciding how to stage it and guiding the others on how to perform it. To start, I was disappointed to be stuck directing rather than acting, but actually, I really got into it – to the point that the afternoon was almost over before I even realized how late it was.

Hal showed up at the Old Row Theatre stage door about an hour before we finished, just as we took a break before performing our scenes for the group. He was promptly adopted by Billie, who was finalizing the lighting for our scenes.

"If your boyfriend's going to hang around here, he might as well come in and make himself useful," Billie said, before giving Hal orders to meet her in the lighting box with two coffees in ten minutes.

"Is she *seriously* dating the homeless guy?" Rina, one of the lookalikes, asked, in the sort of voice that was supposed to be a whisper but really carried across the room. "That's *hilarious.*" I shot her a glare. Lucky for her she wasn't in my group, or I'd have found some way to get my own back.

"Why do they think I'm homeless?" Hal asked, as I pointed him towards the backstage coffee machine.

"Because they're idiots." Then I raised my voice so I could be sure they heard *me*. "And even if you were, it takes a special sort of awful to think that the nation's housing crisis is funny." Huh. Sometimes I even sounded like Alice when I wasn't properly trying.

Rina muttered something about me under her breath. I ignored her.

I sent Hal off to the lighting box and headed back to the stage to watch the performances. I felt a slight pang that the others were up on the stage for the first time, while I sat in the wings watching. But they did well, and a warm sort of pride filled me as I applauded my group louder than all the others.

Besides, I reminded myself, afterwards Vincent would be announcing who'd be performing which pieces in the showcase at the end of the following week.

He'd been watching us all day Monday and that day to decide who was the best fit for which part. I'd made an extra effort as director to demonstrate how I thought my actors should perform certain lines whenever he was in earshot. I hoped that was enough to secure me one of the best parts.

It wasn't.

In a move I should have predicted but hadn't, Vincent gave all the best parts to Tuppence and her friends. I rolled my eyes as I got handed the script for my monologue. A boring speech made by some queen *centuries* ago, that had nothing to do with anything. Not an obvious fit for *Heatherside*. And not even as much fun as directing.

It didn't matter. Natural talent would show through, right? And if I, as the daughter of *two* actors, didn't have natural talent, who would?

Of course, that didn't stop me moaning to Hal about it all the way home.

Thursday, I was all prepared to go window-shopping for the afternoon, mostly to make me feel better about the stupid monologue, but Hal had other plans.

"We have a science camp day trip this afternoon. Have you ever been to the Old Operating Theatre?" he asked, with just a little too much enthusiasm.

"No. And probably for good reasons."

Hal laughed. "It's my favourite museum in London. Just fascinating. You should come with us!"

"Don't you think your camp leaders might notice an extra person on their trip?" Billie might have welcomed Hal at the theatre, especially since he'd proved actually useful on the tech side, but I couldn't imagine science camp being so accepting.

"It's a public museum," Hal pointed out. "I can just meet you there."

"OK." I was willing to give anything a try once. And I probably wouldn't faint. As long as no one was coming at me with any needles...

Hal obviously sensed my lack of conviction. "And it's not far from Shakespeare's Globe. We can head there after, if you like?"

"Sounds like a plan." Maybe the ghost of William Shakespeare would help me find the motivation I needed for my showcase piece.

Whenever I'd come to London with my parents, we'd mostly been up in the West End, perusing the shops on Oxford Street or watching street performers in Covent Garden. I'd explored the South Bank when we'd been to see something at the National Theatre, but rarely made it further than the London Eye or Borough Market for lunch.

The Old Operating Theatre had definitely not been on my radar.

After spending an hour looking at ancient medical stuff, and hearing Hal's friend Toby describe how doctors used to saw off people's legs and arms without anaesthetic, I was done. In fact, my head was spinning and my stomach felt disconnected from the rest of my body. Just as I started to worry that I *might* faint after all (how embarrassing would *that* be?) Hal's teacher declared the trip over, and Hal raced across to tell him he was heading home from here.

We left a few science history diehards obsessing over some old bottles of poison and headed out towards the river, where I gratefully sucked in what passed for fresh air.

"Not planning on changing careers to become a

doctor, then?" Hal asked, amused.

"Definitely not," I confirmed. "What about you? You fancy the medical profession?"

Hal shrugged. "I don't know yet. I like science – especially biology and chemistry. But I reckon I might like the research side more than the practical."

"Like your dad?"

"Yeah, maybe. My mum's a surgeon at the best hospital in London, and I know she'd like it if I followed in *her* footsteps. I hate having to choose which parent to make happy. Maybe that's why I hang out at the Old Operating Theatre so often. Trying to figure out which path to take."

"It's an *interesting* place to try to figure things out." How he could think at all with all those torture devices around was beyond me.

We ambled along by the river, up back towards the Globe.

"What about you?" Hal asked. "What are you going to be when you grow up?"

I rolled my eyes – *such* a little kid question.

"Can't you guess? I *am* going to follow in my parents' footsteps."

Hal looked confused for a moment. "Biologist? No, wait, that's the real Alice."

I smiled smugly. "The fact you'd forgotten that I'm not her backs up my case for my future career."

"Spy? Professional conman?" Hal guessed.

"Actor," I said. "Like my parents."

"So that's why the theatre course was such a big deal."

"Well, yeah. Obviously. Why did you *think* I was doing it?"

Hal shrugged. "I guess I always think of that sort of thing – drama and art and stuff – as hobbies. Not something people actually do as jobs."

"Somebody has to," I pointed out. "Or what would you watch on TV or go to the cinema to see? Not everyone makes it big, I know. But *some* people do. And I will too." Of that much, I was certain.

The Globe was spectacular – a replica of how Shakespeare's theatre would have looked in his day. There were no performances scheduled that afternoon, so I managed to talk my way on to a tour of the actual stage too.

It felt totally different to the small, shabby stage at the Old Row. As I stood in the middle, staring out at the tiers of benches up in the circle, and the standing-room-only area in front of the stage, I tried to imagine acting here.

"I guess this whole summer is just playing another part to you." Hal appeared beside me unexpectedly, breaking through my daydream. "Are you ever going to come clean? Tell Mabel and Jon the truth about who you are?"

"Why on earth would I do that?" At least, not until I was safely back home with my parents. Then I'd tell them everything, to show them how much I didn't need them to plan my life for me.

"Guilt, maybe?" Hal suggested.

I didn't feel guilty. Alice and I had both taken control of our own lives, for the first time ever. What was so bad about that?

"Even if I wanted to, I couldn't tell Mabel the truth now." I moved towards the edge of the stage, sitting on the edge and jumping down to where the audience stood. Turning, I took in the view of the stage from here, my neck aching at looking up even for a few minutes. How great must the performances be to keep the audience doing that for hours? I loved the thought of being part of that. Of creating something that held people completely enthralled.

Hal jumped down after me. "Why not?"

"Because it would screw things up for Alice. She's having a great time over in Italy. Why would I ruin that for her?" Not to mention that *I* was having a pretty good time here in London too. I mean, Alice's descriptions of the village by my Aunt Sofia's farmhouse sounded cool but the city suited me much better. Other than staring at Antonio, it didn't seem like there was much to do there.

"So you're doing this for Alice. Totally altruistic, right?"

I gave Hal my widest, brightest smile. "That's me. Completely selfless."

He shook his head. "I hope she appreciates all we're doing over here to keep your secret."

"Oh, she definitely does," I assured him. "I mean, she'll probably want to thank you personally when she gets back. Maybe even take you out."

"Like on a date?" Hal asked.

I smiled mysteriously. "Maybe. Maybe."

ALICE

We turned a corner and suddenly the steady sound of the river turned into something more like the crash of waves against the sea wall in a storm.

The path was too narrow here for us to walk side by side. Luca had been in front so far but now he stepped into the greenery at the side of the path to let me go first. I smiled my thanks, my heartbeat kicking up a gear as I realized I was really, really here.

I sucked in a deep breath and clenched my hands into fists at my sides, nails digging into my palms. And then the waterfall came into view.

"Oh, wow." Luca whispered the words. He was so close his mouth was almost against my ear, so that I heard them anyway.

Cascata della Fuga was the most beautiful sight I'd ever seen. Forget the oceans of the world, with their mysterious depths. Forget Antonio. Forget everything else, in fact.

It started high above our heads, a surge of water

flinging itself off the top of a cliff and cascading down the rock face.

"I can't decide if it looks angry or determined," I said.

Luca looked at me as if I'd lost my mind. "I was just thinking it was beautiful."

"That too," I agreed.

"Want to get closer?" he asked. "There's an information board over there."

I nodded, and we continued down the path.

"What does it say?" I asked.

"It's the legend of Cascata della Fuga," Luca said, scanning the board. "Huh. I didn't know that. The story goes that some girl was supposed to marry an old guy she hated, but at the last minute a giant bird showed up and picked her up in his claws, carrying her away to the other side of the country. It dropped her here and her tears of relief grew into this waterfall."

We both looked up at the fierce, forceful cascade of water.

"Legend is that if you stand under the falls and shout your fears and worries into the water, they'll be carried away by the river and never bother you again."

"That's basically what Mum said. Well, apart from

the 'stand *under* the falls' part." Seemed to me that if I had to stand under that I'd have bigger worries.

"No, it's OK." Luca pointed to a small box on the information board with a map. "There's caves behind the falls. Come on, let's see if we can find the way in."

He was off before I could agree – or disagree. I followed more slowly.

"Are you ready?" Luca yelled. But either he didn't hear me say, "No," or he didn't listen. Instead, he gave me a small push forwards on the damp, muddy path that wound between the rocks and behind the falling water. Biting the inside of my cheek, I picked my way carefully along towards the hidden cave.

Then I looked back.

"Aren't you coming?" Part of me didn't want him to, because then I could shout whatever I wanted without being heard. But part of me really didn't want to do this alone.

Luca shook his head. "We came here for *you* to do this. I'll wait here," he yelled.

Right. Doing this alone, then.

A few more steps and the path widened out as it became pure rock underfoot. One more step and I was inside the cool and damp of the cave.

How did this work, then? Did I just … stand close

to the edge and shout? There were no safety railings so I could get so close that I was almost in the water itself...

I took a step back, just enough to be sure my trainers wouldn't lose their grip and send me flying. Then I looked up into the cascading water, feeling the rhythm of it thrumming through my body like a drumbeat.

"I miss my mum," I said tentatively, the words swallowed up by the water. "I hate being scared all the time."

Nothing changed, really. Except that more words started bubbling up inside me.

Glancing quickly to my side to make sure Luca hadn't followed me, I shouted out my biggest secret.

"I'm Alice. Not Willa. I am Alice Wright!"

My name echoed in my head, and reverberated through the waves.

I grinned to myself. And then I began to shout.

I can't tell you exactly what I said but I felt the words leaving, taking their worries with them.

I threw out my worries, my fears, my pain. Mum. Dad, in Australia. Mabel. The future. Willa. Italy and London. School. Antonio. Luca. The lies I was telling. The life I'd go back to. Being Alice again. Not being Alice again.

Moving on.

Luca told me later that I was there for a full twenty minutes, so I guess there must have been more. Fears I didn't even know I had, pouring out of me and into the waterfall.

When I'd finished, my whole body felt lighter but I was exhausted, and my throat was raw.

I stumbled back out of the cave, feeling my way along the path with one hand on the cliff face, to where Luca was waiting for me.

"You get what you needed?" he asked, looking concerned.

I smiled, almost delirious with the relief of letting it all go. "I did."

WILLA

Just when I thought the plan was going *perfectly*, trouble appeared from an unexpected source.

My own body.

Since my periods started, about a year and a half ago, they'd been pretty unremarkable. I was still waiting for them to settle into any sort of a regular cycle, but on the plus side they didn't last too long and I didn't get really awful cramps like my friend Noemi did. (Tara always said she was milking it for the attention, but I'd seen her clutching her stomach and begging the school nurse for painkillers, so I didn't think so.)

Unfortunately, not having a regular cycle meant I had no idea when it was going to show up. Still, this was one area in my life where I believed in being prepared, so I always made sure I had a tampon in my bag – and I'd packed a whole box of them, plus overnight pads, for my trip away this summer.

So when I went to the loo on Friday morning and saw blood, I didn't panic.

Until I remembered that all my stuff – including my box of tampons – was in Italy, with Alice.

Then I panicked.

My heart racing, I checked the tiny bathroom cabinet for supplies. Shower gel, a spare toothbrush, and some apricot facial scrub. That was it.

Oh God. I was going to have to talk to Mabel. About periods.

Asking Mabel if she had a tampon I could borrow until I could get to the shop to buy my own was even worse than having to ask my *dad* to go to the shop and buy me sanitary products.

"Alice? Are you OK in there?" Mabel asked, knocking on the bathroom door. Apparently I'd been a while.

"Um, yeah. Fine." I shoved some toilet paper in my knickers as a temporary fix, flushed the loo, and opened the door. "I just… I got my period."

Mabel's face turned white, then pink, then she clapped her hands together and said, "Oh, Alice! Your dad told me you hadn't yet, but we figured it couldn't be long, so I made sure I had some supplies in ready. Don't worry. Wait here!"

She started to dash off towards her bedroom, then turned back and gave me a really tight hug, before disappearing again. I sat down on the closed toilet seat and waited. I couldn't exactly tell her this *wasn't* my first period – not when it should be Alice's. I'd have to message Alice later and explain, in case her dad called to check that she was OK with it all.

Yeah, this was really weird now.

"Now, it's important for you to figure out what you're comfortable with – what your flow is like, how your body reacts, your own cycle and signs, that sort of thing. But to start you off, I have this."

Mabel handed me a box decorated with brightly coloured paper, and I opened it gingerly. She sat on the side of the bath to watch me.

"This is … great," I said, with a weak smile, as I surveyed the contents.

Four packs of sanitary towels – for light, medium and heavy flow, plus overnight towels. A leaflet entitled 'Listen to your body, learn your cycle'. A large bar of chocolate, a book called *You're a Big Girl Now* with an awful cartoon of a nervous-looking girl on the front, and a small, shell-shaped purse which, when I opened it, was stuffed with ibuprofen.

No tampons. I guess she thought Alice would be more comfortable with pads, starting off. Urgh. I hated wearing pads during the day. I'd pick up some tampons for when I was out.

Mabel leaned towards me. "If you have any questions at all, or even if you just want to moan about cramps, I'm here for you. I know this must be so hard for you, doing this – growing up, I mean – without your mum here. And I'd never presume to even think about taking her place, for any of it. But… I'd like to be a friend, Alice, if I can. And a good friend is always there with a shoulder to cry on, an ear to listen, and a big bar of chocolate. OK?"

I actually felt a little bit teary at her words – and *my* mum wasn't even dead. Stupid hormones.

"OK," I said, and Mabel smiled.

"Then I'll leave you to it. Unless you need me to show you—"

"No!" I interrupted quickly. "No, I'm fine. Thank you."

The last thing I needed was Alice's possible step-mother showing me how to use a sanitary pad. That was definitely *not* what I'd come to London for.

Tuppence and her hangers-on were particularly annoying at the theatre that day – or maybe I was just more easily annoyable. Having scored the best scenes and monologues between them, they were now demanding the lion's share of attention in sorting out their scenery, costumes and lighting for the showcase. Billie looked run ragged – and relieved when Hal showed up at five to help.

"Any chance you can help out a bit more next week?" she asked, and Hal looked to me for guidance. I shrugged.

"I guess so," he said. "My science camp finished today, so I've got some free time."

Plus if he was at the theatre with me, there was no chance of Mabel running into him somewhere and wondering why he wasn't still at science camp when I was. Perfect. Well, as long as she didn't try to visit the camp at the other university site again. But when I'd asked a few casual questions, it didn't seem like she went over there too often, so we were probably safe.

The course showcase was to be a combination of short scenes performed in small groups and individual monologues. We had some of the classics in there – the three witches from *Macbeth* (played, appropriately enough, by the three lookalikes), some classic *Romeo and Juliet* between Tuppence and Ryan, the selfie mirror guy who, it turned out, had already been a child star in the West End. And there was modern stuff too – even a song or two from the musicals. Almost all of which was more fun than my dying queen monologue. Not that I was complaining. Much. Or at least, not when Vincent could hear me. (Hal, on the other hand, had heard *all* about it.)

Anyway, we only had three full afternoons to learn, prepare and rehearse the material, find costumes and sets, and sort the tech for our scenes. Vincent claimed that doing it all ourselves gave us a well-rounded overview of the theatre experience. I just figured he couldn't be bothered to do it himself. After he assigned pieces on the second day, he'd mostly been wandering around our rehearsal spaces, drinking coffee, and imparting anecdotes from his glory days.

I was starting to wonder who he'd paid to write all those glowing reports of his course, to be honest. He wasn't even directing us!

Hal and I headed home together at six as usual, both ready for the weekend. Mabel texted to say that she was running late and would meet me at the flat, so I said goodbye to Hal at the Tube station.

It was strange letting myself into the empty flat, but before I'd even had a chance to shove my bag in my room, Mabel was at the door, a large bakery box in her hands. And she was grinning.

I had a bad feeling about this.

"Hey, Alice! How are you? How are you feeling? Did science camp go OK today?"

"It was fine." I stared at the box in her hands. Suddenly, I had an image of a cake iced with the words 'Congratulations on your first period, Alice!'

No. Mabel wouldn't. Would she?

I followed her into the kitchen, warily.

"Fancy a slice of cake before we decide where to order dinner from?" She placed the cake on the kitchen table. "Since it's a special day, and everything."

Oh God, she *would*.

"That would be lovely," I said, trying to prepare my face not to wince when I saw it.

Slowly, she opened the box to reveal...

A perfectly ordinary round cake with cream cheese icing. Thank *God*.

Then she picked up a knife and sliced through it to reveal the bright red sponge inside.

"Red velvet cake," she said, giggling. "I couldn't resist. Sorry. It just seemed so appropriate!"

I couldn't help myself. I burst into giggles too as I took the plate from her.

"At least there aren't tampon-shaped candles," I said, between bursts of laughter.

And after that, we were both laughing too hard to eat the cake for a good five minutes.

ALICE

"Didn't you have anything you wanted to let go of at the waterfall?" I asked Luca, as we waited for the first bus that would take us back to Lunice. "No worries or fears?"

Luca shrugged and looked away. "Too many for one little river to deal with." I flinched. I should have known that. And it only made me wonder again what Luca's life had been like before he came to live with Sofia and Mattias.

Maybe one day soon, I would feel brave enough to ask.

"Why did you come, then? If you weren't going to shout into the water or anything."

"Told you. I knew it was important to you, and I figured you'd need the help." He flashed me a smile as the bus pulled up beside us. "Besides, it was nice to get away from the farmhouse and everyone, just for a little bit. Don't you think?"

"Yeah. It was." In fact, it had been nice just spending time with Luca, and hearing a bit more about his life.

I just wished I could have told him more about mine.

We were halfway back to Lunice when I realized something was wrong.

The first sign was the driver swearing loudly in Italian (Luca had taught me those words, rather than Rosa). The other passengers on the bus started muttering, as the bus began to slow.

"Why are we stopping?" I peered out of the window.

Luca looked up from his phone – he'd been trying to get reception on it ever since we left the waterfall. "No idea. Wait, hang on…"

He jumped up from his seat so he could peer through the front windscreen.

"Pigs." Luca dropped into the seat beside me again. "There's two pigs sitting in the road."

"Seriously?" I got to my feet to check for myself. Sure enough, there were two large pigs stopped right in the centre of the narrow road.

The bus driver leaned heavily on the horn, sending the loud noise echoing off the hill on one side of the road, out over the valley on the other.

The pigs didn't move.

Luca and I were both at the front of the bus now, watching the pigs not moving.

"They're big for pigs," I commented.

I leaned further forwards to try to see, just as the bus driver beeped the horn again. It made me jump but the pigs didn't flinch.

Suddenly, Luca's phone started beeping and vibrating in his hand. "Reception at last!" His gleeful expression soon fell, though. "Wait, fourteen missed calls and eight text messages?"

I pulled out my phone. "Sofia … and Mattias?" I had three missed calls and a handful of texts from them too.

"And Antonio," Luca added. He swiped at the screen, and I watched his face go pale. "My grandparents are visiting. They arrived this morning… Sofia's been trying to get hold of us ever since."

"Your … grandparents?" I didn't know he even *had* any family that might visit. And if he had grandparents, why wasn't he living with them?

But Luca wasn't listening – he was banging on the bus doors, until the driver – yelling more words Rosa *definitely* hadn't taught me – opened them, and Luca raced out on to the road.

"Luca!" I ran after him.

He was waving his arms at the pigs, shouting at them in Italian. I could guess his meaning, though. The animals stared back at him, completely unaffected.

"We've got to get them to move, Willa." He sounded desperate. "I've *got* to get back."

"We'll miss our bus back to Tusello," I realized.

"And then we'll really be in for it."

Luca's miserable expression made my mind up for me. He'd come all this way to help me find a waterfall. The least I could do was shift two pigs to help him get home again.

"Maybe if we do it together."

We both started shouting and waving at them, but the pigs just looked more confused than ever.

I took a deep breath, got behind the biggest one and started pushing. "Come on, you stupid, stinking, overweight, ridiculous, stubborn *pig!*" The last word came out as a bit of a shriek as the animal suddenly chose *that* moment to finally move – sending me sprawling across the road, straight into something so disgusting it could only be pig poo.

I pushed myself up to my hands and knees as the other pig casually followed its friend out of the road, for all the world like they'd just been taking a break. The bus driver beeped the horn again – presumably to hurry us back on to the bus, and it was only then that I looked up at Luca, who had his hand over his mouth, trying (unsuccessfully) to stifle his laughter.

I rubbed my filthy hands on my jeans and waited for the familiar heat of embarrassment to flood my body – but for the first time ever, it didn't come.

Instead, a bubble of laughter started in my throat and burst out of my mouth. Which set Luca off, until we were both giggling uncontrollably.

Because it *was* funny. It was *hilarious*.

The bus driver beeped the horn again, and Luca held out a hand to pull me up, still laughing.

"Come on. We need to get back. We can think of an excuse as to why you're covered in pig poo on the way. I don't think Sofia and Mattias will believe we got held up by pigs on the main road between Lunice and Tusello."

"Probably not," I agreed, between giggles.

WILLA

"I'm so sorry I've been so taken up with work this week." Mabel cast me an apologetic look in the mirror by the front door as she threaded her earrings in. "I hope tonight will make up for it. You look lovely, by the way."

Standing behind her, I shrugged myself into Alice's best cardigan, and looked down at my outfit.

It could be worse. At least it wasn't the five-year-old's party dress.

Mabel had been pretty happy to leave me to my own devices for most of the week. Every night I'd given her a recap of science camp – as told to me by Hal on the train home – and that seemed to satisfy her. But tonight she had plans for us – theatre plans. And apparently that required dressing up.

I'd actually opened my mouth to tell her that people didn't dress up for the theatre any more. Then I'd shut it again and gone to dig out a respectable skirt and top to wear for the evening, just like Alice would have done.

Sometimes being Alice was no fun at all. At least at the theatre I got to be Willa.

"I should take a photo to send to your dad." Mabel rummaged in her bag for her phone, while my heart started a panicked thumping beat.

"No time for that," I said, yanking open the door. "We don't want to be late, do we?"

"Of course not!" Mabel's eyes were wide at the very idea. "Remind me to take one later though, will you?"

"Absolutely."

Mabel had picked a play I'd never heard of, but it apparently had got a great review in the Sunday papers. Mabel obviously wasn't a theatre fan, exactly, but 'a night at the theatre' was right there on her 'things Alice might like to do in London' list, and so we had to go.

Weirdly, though, it was nice to spend an evening with Mabel. She *was* nice, even if I didn't talk much to Alice about that. Mabel was totally unlike my mum, and I had no way of knowing how she measured up to Alice's. But as a room mate for the summer, she was OK.

We had dinner together in Covent Garden, then walked across Leicester Square to the theatre. Of course everyone else within a decade of my age was

227

wearing jeans, and I rolled my eyes and glared at Alice's boring beige skirt. But I got that Mabel had wanted this to be a special evening. And at least the red strapless top I'd bought on our shopping trip had brightened things up a bit. (With the cardigan on, Mabel didn't even seem worried about what my dad would think of it.)

Handing over our tickets at the entrance, we were directed through the stalls to our seats. Mabel was engrossed in the programme, so I gazed around, taking in the theatre and the theatregoers and...

I'd know that orange jacket anywhere.

Just a few rows in front and half a row over sat Vincent Paloma. Star of stage and screen, director of drama summer camp, and one of the few people in London who would absolutely, definitely know that I was Willa, not Alice.

My heart raced as I watched him take his seat, his partner beside him.

Any moment now he was going to turn round and see me. I swallowed hard, my cheeks hot and my hands clammy.

Any moment... Now.

Vincent started to turn and I did the only thing I could think of. I hid.

"Alice? What are you doing down there?" Mabel peered at me as I scrabbled on the floor by our seats.

"Um, just dropped my phone. I was putting it on silent and it slipped out of my hand." I carefully got back up and sat in my seat, keeping my hair across my face. After a few moments, I risked a peek through my hair and saw that Vincent had sat down again, facing the stage.

As long as he kept his focus on the play, I'd be fine.

Finally, the lights in the theatre started to dim, and my shoulders relaxed. I was safe until the interval, at least.

By the time the lights went up again for the interval, I still wasn't sure what the play was about, but I did at least have a plan.

"Do you want an ice cream?" Mabel asked.

Perfect. "Yes, please. I'm just going to pop to the loo."

Queues for theatre toilets are always ridiculous, so I was still standing outside in the hallway waiting my turn when Vincent entered the bar from the other side. My eyes widened as I realized he was heading my way – which was when I spotted the table full of drinks with name cards next to them. In particular, the one that said 'Paloma' on it.

Well, if he spotted me, I could talk to him as Willa, get away as quickly as possible.

It would still be absolutely fine.

Or it would have been if Mabel hadn't suddenly popped up, just as Vincent caught sight of me and smiled.

"I don't have any cash on me, but apparently I can get ice cream from the bar with a card," Mabel said. "So I'm just going to—"

"Actually, I'm still full from dinner," I said, turning quickly so my back was to Vincent Paloma. "Let's get back to our seats. I think the play's about to start again." I started bustling Mabel towards the door back into the main theatre.

"Did they ring the bell already?" the woman in front of me in the queue asked, blocking our path. "I didn't hear it."

"I think I did," her companion said. "Or maybe it was my hearing aid."

"*I* didn't hear it," Mabel complained, but I gave her another nudge towards the door anyway. "Are you sure you don't want ice cream?"

"Absolutely sure. And that was definitely the bell," I said, loud enough that the whole queue could hear.

That was all it took to get everyone moving. All grumbling about theatre toilets and short intervals, suddenly everyone was abandoning the queue, downing interval drinks, and pushing their way past everyone else – and, most importantly, getting between me and the man who might have blown my cover.

My phone started vibrating in my pocket, but I ignored it. Probably just a text from Alice, anyway, about that road trip she and Luca had been planning. She could fill me in later. I still had the second half of the play to get through.

And I didn't even get any ice cream.

ALICE

After stopping for pig-related delays, we missed the final bus home and Mattias had to drive to Lunice to collect us. He raised his eyebrows at the state of me but he didn't ask any questions. I thought this was a good thing, until I realized he was just leaving it to Sofia to grill us about later.

Luca and I stuck to our story, though. We'd cleaned off the worst of my clothes in the bus-station toilets, so while I still looked a mess, we figured we might get away without having to claim we'd visited another farm. Instead, we just told Sofia that we'd lost track of time, and our phones had both lost signal. Which was sort of true.

The worst part was that Luca's grandparents had already gone by the time we got home.

"They said they'd try to come back tomorrow," Sofia said, with a sigh and a meaningful look at Luca. "So you'd better get a good night's sleep."

He just nodded, then headed for his room.

Sofia turned and headed back into the kitchen.

She hadn't told *me* to go to bed exactly, so I followed.

"We really are very sorry." I boosted myself up on to one of the kitchen stools, watching as she made herself her customary evening peppermint tea.

"I know." She sighed again. "It was just … unfortunate it happened to be today. And that Luca's grandparents didn't give us any notice that they were coming."

I frowned. "Why *did* they come, exactly?"

Sighing, Sofia pulled out a stool and sat down at the counter, her cup of tea steaming in front of her. "With fostering… I take in the children while they need me. Sometimes their parents aren't capable of looking after them any longer, sometimes they just need some time to get things together again. Sometimes there are no other relatives, and sometimes relatives come forward and offer to help."

"Is that what happened this time?" I asked.

Sofia waggled her head from side to side, half yes and half no. "Originally we hoped that Luca and the others would be able to go back to their mother, sooner or later. But eventually it became clear that wouldn't be an option."

I wanted to ask why, but I knew it wasn't Sofia's place to tell me that story.

"Their grandparents live in England. They looked after them on and off when they were younger, I believe," Sofia went on. "In between other respite and foster care. But then when their parents split up, and their mother moved them back to Italy with her, they lost contact for a while."

"That must have been hard," I said.

"Anyway, the authorities eventually managed to get in contact with them through the British social services, to see if they might be able to live with them full time. But they were about to leave the country, on an extended trip to stay with relatives in Australia. Celebrating their retirement, I believe."

I was starting to get a bad feeling about this.

"But they're back now?" I asked.

Sofia nodded. "And they decided to come and see the children. Without warning, without giving me time to prepare them." She sounded far more annoyed than she had when Luca had been there.

"To see if they can go and live with them again? In Britain?"

"Yes."

Did they even want to? Luca loved it here, I knew. Rosa adored Sofia and Mattias. And even Antonio... Sofia had taken him to London to look at universities.

She'd helped him plan his future.

Why would they want to go?

"Willa…" Sofia sighed again, before pulling out her phone. "Are you happy here? I thought that you were enjoying your summer, but…"

"I am!" I jumped in quickly. "Really, Aunt Sofia, this has been the best summer. Today was just a mistake, that's all."

"I wasn't talking about today." She turned her phone screen towards me, and I stared at it, trying to understand what I was looking at.

Willa's Instagram feed. With a photo of London, and a caption saying she wished she was there.

#italianhell

Willa!

I tried to imagine what excuse Willa would make. "Oh, that?" I gave a weak laugh. "I didn't know you were on Instagram or I wouldn't have posted it."

"But that's how you feel, isn't it?"

I shook my head. "Not at all. I was just … trying to get at my parents. You know, for sending me here without asking, when I was supposed to be at a theatre course in London. Even though I'm *loving* being here with you… I'm still a bit mad at them both."

Sofia didn't look entirely convinced. "You're sure?"

"Very." I gave an enthusiastic nod. Then, I wrapped my arms round her, hoped she couldn't smell pig poo, and hugged her. "Really. Thank you for having me this summer. I wouldn't want to be anywhere else."

And then I went for a shower before bed.

"How long has it been since you've seen your grandparents?" I asked Luca the next morning, as I sat on the wall by the donkey stables, watching him feed Achilles and Hercules. We were both under instructions to stay within earshot and keep clean today.

"Years." Luca flashed me a grin. "Honestly, I'm not even sure Rosa remembers them. After we came home to Italy … we never saw my father's side of the family again."

I finally summoned the nerve to ask. "Where's your dad?"

Luca shrugged. "He … left. Eventually. Mum would never say where he went. Maybe his parents will tell us."

He was playing it pretty cool, but there was a thread of something – anticipation, I suppose – in everything he did that morning. He couldn't stay still, rushing from animal to animal with food and water, brushing the donkeys, always keeping his hands busy. As the morning wore on, the excitement only grew.

And so did the bad feeling in the pit of my stomach.

I didn't want to get in the way of this family reunion. More than ever, I knew it wasn't my place to be there today – even if I really *had* been Sofia's niece. So I hid up in my room as soon as Mattias called from the olive grove to say that their car had just turned into the driveway. Of course, it just so happened that my room looked out over the front of the house, so I was able to stand at the window and watch as Luca's grandparents climbed out of the car.

They were younger than I'd expected, given that they had a seventeen-year-old grandson in Antonio. They were dressed smartly, but their shoulders were stiff, and when Rosa jumped forwards to hug her grandmother it took a long moment for the woman to hug her back.

Antonio shook hands with them both, and Luca followed suit – although I suspected he wanted to behave more like Rosa had.

I let the curtain fall, and pulled out a book to keep me occupied during the visit.

Ninety minutes later, I heard their car pull away again. Cautiously, I made my way down the stairs to where I found Rosa sobbing in Sofia's arms in the kitchen. Antonio, stony-faced, walked past me and out of the back door. I heard the familiar thud of the axe as he cut firewood. Luca was nowhere to be seen.

"What happened?" I whispered to Mattias, as he shut the kitchen door.

He shrugged. "Apparently they discussed it all last night, after their visit yesterday. They decided that don't have space for three children in their lives."

"Is this because Luca and I were late home?" Was this my fault? Had taking me to that stupid waterfall ruined Luca's chances of getting his family back?

But Mattias shook his head. "I don't think so. I think they'd already made their minds up before they even made it into the country."

They hadn't come to be reunited. They'd come to say goodbye.

Poor Luca. I couldn't imagine how he must feel. He'd been so panicked about missing them yesterday, and now...

Would he blame me? Part of my brain spun with the worry, but I pushed it aside. None of this was about me. It was about my friend. And I had a feeling he might need me.

And so I headed out to find Luca.

It took me a while; I tried the donkeys first, then the olive grove, before I realized he'd already told me where he'd be. His favourite hiding place.

Wishing I'd brought snacks, I made my way up to the village, to the section of the old wall where we'd eaten gelato on my first day in Italy.

Luca sat huddled against the wall, not looking out at the sea, not eating gelato, and not looking at all like the excited boy he'd been that morning. I lowered myself to sit beside him.

"Want to talk about it?" I asked softly.

Luca shook his head. "What is there to say? They don't want us. Same as everyone else."

My heart hurt for him. And I thought I'd been abandoned by my dad, while he worked this summer. That was nothing like what Luca was going through.

"This is why I couldn't shout it all out at the waterfall," he said angrily. "I *can't* let go. I have to remember everything that's happened to me. All the people who've let me down. My dad, taking everything out on my mum until Antonio stood between them. He left when I called the police. And Mum… She couldn't cope. She chose escape over us too.

She checked out of everything. Apparently she's in some rehab place now… And now *those people* today."

"They don't deserve you," I said fiercely.

"What about what I deserve, Willa?" Luca asked, looking up at me. "And Rosa and Antonio?"

There wasn't anything I could say to that.

"I have to remember," he said again. "That way, it'll hurt less next time it happens."

I wanted to cry for him, for everything he'd been through.

He'd taken me to the waterfall. He'd helped me let go of all the things that were holding me back. And I wanted so badly to be able to do the same for him.

"It's not about forgetting," I said, thinking of my mum. "It's about moving forwards."

"What is there for me to move forwards to, though?" Luca asked. "I'm unwanted, remember?"

"Sofia wants you. And Mattias." And me, I wanted to say. But I'd be leaving soon. And I wasn't even the person he thought I was.

"Do they? Maybe they just want the money they get for looking after us."

"They want you," I said firmly. "Or they wouldn't make you such an important part of their family."

"But we're not, are we?" Luca looked up at me, his

eyes bright with tears. "None of us. We're not their blood – not the way you are. You're Sofia's niece, you belong here. We're just visiting."

I felt cold at his words. I *wasn't* blood. But how could I tell him that now?

"That makes it more important. They *chose* to have you here. Chose to let you into their lives – not because you're related to them, but because they *wanted* you here with them. That matters a lot more than blood."

And it did, I realized. So I wasn't really Willa Andrews, but I *was* the person who Luca had spent the summer with. Had made friends with. Had comforted and talked to the night of the festival. Had taken to Cascata della Fuga. Had chased pigs with.

And I would help him get through this too.

"They're idiots if they don't want the three of you with them," I whispered. Then I jumped to my feet. "Come on. I'll buy you a gelato."

WILLA

The next week was manic. When we weren't at the theatre, rehearsing and working on sets and costumes, I was practising my lines with Hal in coffee shops and parks across London, while we stayed out of Mabel's way and pretended we were still at science camp.

Since I was one of the few people performing on my own, rehearsing was a bit more boring for me than the groups doing scenes. Still, I liked being at the theatre, and some of the others asked for my help or advice while they were rehearsing too. Apparently my directorial skills were in high demand after the small group scenes we'd done the week before. (Ours had *clearly* been the best, so I wasn't very surprised.)

I'd also been dragged in to perform in a second scene with Tuppence and Ryan, after Rina had come down with tonsillitis over the weekend, so now I had *two* parts to prepare for. And I had to deal with Tuppence trying to boss me about.

"This is *my* scene, remember, so we do it *my* way," she said, the first time I stood in. "We all know I have the best shot at getting a place at that audition, and the last thing I need is you amateurs screwing it up for me."

Ryan and I exchanged a look. I got the feeling even he was getting fed up with Tuppence's theatrics. And I couldn't help wonder why she needed this audition anyway – unless her fancy stage school didn't think she was good enough to put forwards for *Heatherside* the normal ways.

I stood back as Tuppence started the scene. I let her get out her first three lines before saying, "And you're sure you want to do it like *that*?"

Things had been going downhill ever since.

"You could have said no when Vincent asked," Hal pointed out, as I moaned about Tuppence while we took half an hour out to lounge in St James's Park on Tuesday afternoon.

"And miss out on having a second chance to wow the casting agent at the showcase? No, thank you. Besides, Tuppence got all the best scenes."

"So, this casting agent," Hal said. "What are they casting *for* exactly?"

"How do you not know this already?" I sat up straight in amazement. "You've been at the theatre all week!"

"And all I've heard any of you talking about is how

you need your costume to be more flattering, and the lighting isn't showing off your best side."

He had a point. "It's the casting agent for *Heatherside*," I said. "They're adding a new family to the show, and they're looking for actors to play two teenage children."

"And they're going to choose from you lot?"

I ignored Hal's doubtful tone. "No." Even if that *was* what I'd thought from the course message group, before Billie explained. "The casting agent is going to watch our showcase and, if she likes us, she'll choose the best two or three of us to attend the proper audition for *Heatherside* the next day."

"Huh. And that's why you did all this? To try to get a part on a soap opera?"

"Every great acting career has to start somewhere! And anyway, don't knock *Heatherside*," I said "My dad's an actor on the show, you realize."

"Right. Sorry."

"That's OK. But a part in the show *would* be a great first step on the acting ladder." I plucked a few blades of grass from the ground beside me, weaving them together.

"But that's not the only reason you want it?" Hal asked.

When did he get so perceptive?

"I guess it's for my dad too. Since he left… I don't get to see him much. But if I got the part, I'd see him at work every day." And his new girlfriend, I supposed. But I didn't think that was going to last long, anyway. Mum was right – this was his midlife crisis. I just wanted him to get over it and remember he had a daughter.

"I get that. I don't see my mum much these days, either. She always seems to be in surgery… Wait. The audition's on a Saturday? How are you going to escape Mabel for that? Assuming you get picked, of course."

"I'll get picked," I said breezily, glad the subject had shifted back to a more comfortable zone. "And I'm sure something will turn up."

Hal flopped on to his back on the grass, one arm over his eyes. "I'm going to end up pretending there's some vital science trip we both need to go on next weekend, aren't I?"

I patted his shoulder. "I knew I could count on you. I'll leave you to figure out the details."

He shifted his arm so he could peer at me past it. "You know I'm not doing this for you, right?"

"I know, I know," I said. "It's all for the love of Alice."

That made him turn bright red. At least, the parts of his face I could still see. "It's not… I'm not… We haven't…"

"Don't get yourself all worked up, Hal." I lay down beside him, resting on one elbow, and dropped my voice to a conspiratorial tone. "As it happens, I think the two of you would be a *perfect* match." Much better than the Antonio guy she'd been crushing on all summer, given what she'd told me.

"Really?" Hal sat bolt upright. "You do?"

"I do. And what's more, I think Alice does too." Well, I thought she would once I convinced her, which was almost the same thing.

Hal blinked at me, obviously stunned into silence by the revelation.

"Just leave the matchmaking to me, Hal. You can focus on setting up my alibi for Saturday."

He nodded enthusiastically, and I silently thanked Alice for whatever power she held over him. Hal's crush had definitely made my scheming this summer a *lot* easier.

"Come on," I said, jumping to my feet and holding out a hand to pull him up. "Break's over. Time to get back to work. I still need to find a costume crown for playing the queen."

ALICE

Good luck with the showcase tomorrow! Or, wait – break a leg. Right?

WILLA

Yeah. Although I'm relying more on talent than luck anyway.

ALICE

And promise me – no more instagram pics.

WILLA

Triple promise.

WILLA

Hal says 'hi' btw. He actually blushed when he asked me to tell you.

ALICE

Oh God. Tell me you're not leading him on?

WILLA

Would I do that?

ALICE
Yes.

ALICE
I mean it, Willa. Do not promise him a date with me, or even hint that I might want to go on one. OK?

WILLA
Yeah, yeah, fine. But I think you're making a mistake. You two would be a *perfect* match.

ALICE
You mean we'd be a convenient match for your plans.

WILLA
That too...

ALICE
Seriously. He's a nice guy, but I really don't think of Hal that way.

ALICE
Like, at all.

The last twenty-four hours before the showcase disappeared in a rush of activity and last minute panic. And then, almost before I knew it, it was Friday afternoon – and time for our showcase. Hal was up in the tech box with Billie, so I was on my own in the wings with the other actors. We all watched as Vincent did a big welcome speech for all the parents and family who'd come to watch us. I couldn't invite Mabel, of course, but it didn't matter. The only person who I cared about was out there in the audience somewhere – the *Heatherside* casting agent.

"You better not screw this up for me, Willa," Tuppence whispered in my ear. I tried to look behind me without actually moving, and spotted Ryan beside her.

"I'm more concerned about you forgetting your lines again like you did in the tech this morning," I murmured back. "Or Ryan spotting a mirror somewhere and being too taken in by his own image to act at all."

I was sure Tuppence had more to say to me, but then the audience were applauding, the curtain was opening, and it was, officially, show time.

Ninety minutes later it was all over.

"You did it!" Hal came racing backstage and threw his arms round me in a huge hug, before I'd even got my costume crown off. Then he let go and shoved a piece of paper in my face. "The casting agent gave Vincent a list of names she wants to see tomorrow and you're on it! Billie sent me to pin it up on the board for you all."

"Let me see that!" Tuppence pushed past the rest of the kids crowding around to snatch the paper from Hal's hand. But not before I'd read my name at the top of it.

I'd done it. I'd actually done it. Deep down, I wasn't sure I'd truly believed I could pull it off. But I had.

Sinking down to sit on the edge of a trunk full of costumes in the dressing room, I barely heard Tuppence's nasal tones reading out the three other names of people who'd been called back – herself, of course, and Ryan and Bethany.

Instead, I pulled my phone from my pocket and started a new text to Alice to tell her the good news.

"We should have a photo!" Tuppence squealed. "The four of us!" Apparently she'd forgotten her concerns about me wrecking things for her, now everything had worked out well.

Before I could object, she grabbed the phone from my hand and tossed it to Hal, who fumbled then caught it. "OK, then. Smile."

He lifted the phone and went to press the home button to switch it over to camera. And it was then, as I watched his face fall, that I realized something terrible.

My text conversation with Alice from the night before, all about Hal, was still on the screen.

"Wait!" I jumped forwards to try to grab it from him, but he held it up higher, where I couldn't reach. I could see him mouthing the words as he read, though, and remembered everything I'd written. Everything *Alice* had written.

Suddenly, his crush didn't seem so funny any more.

"Are we going to take this photo or not?" Tuppence snapped.

Hal looked down at me. "Why not? You all deserve each other." He flipped my phone to camera, and took a shot of the four of us – Tuppence and Ryan smiling brightly, Bethany looking confused, and me staring pleadingly at him.

Then he threw the phone back to me, picked up his

bag, and walked out without another word.

I'd really, really screwed this up.

And I had no idea how to fix it.

"Are you going to go after him?" Bethany asked, and I jerked into action.

"Go after him. Yes." Leaving the others setting up for the after-show party, I dashed down the stairs to the stage door, hoping I could catch him.

But when I got there, Billie stood in front of the door, blocking my way.

"He doesn't want to speak to you, Willa," she said softly. "I don't know what happened between you two, but he asked me to make sure you didn't follow him."

"I need... I need to apologize. Or explain." I darted to one side to try to get past her, but Billie was quicker than me.

"Leave it until tomorrow," Billie advised. "Let him calm down a bit first. Besides, don't you have a party to get to? I heard there's plenty to celebrate."

"I guess." We'd told Mabel there was a get-together for all the science camp people tonight, so she wasn't expecting me home until later.

"Just don't party too hard. You've got the audition tomorrow, remember."

As if I was likely to forget.

She handed me an envelope with my name on, and I opened it to find all the instructions for the audition the next day. I shoved it into my bag to look at later.

I trudged back up the stairs to where I could hear the others celebrating – not just the four of us who'd been invited to the audition, but *all* of us. Our showcase had been a huge success. Hardly anything had gone wrong, and the audience seemed to have enjoyed it. We *all* deserved to celebrate our two weeks at the theatre, especially since it might be the last time some of us ever saw each other.

"Willa! Get in here!" Daisy – who'd been in my group when I was directing, and asked for my help with her own showcase piece – appeared in the doorway at the top of the stairs, beckoning me up. "Come on! We're celebrating!"

Billie was right. I *should* enjoy the party. I'd worked hard for this, I deserved to celebrate. Even if Hal was upset about a few stupid text messages.

By the time I reached Daisy at the top of the stairs, I'd managed to convince myself that Hal was overreacting and that it would all be fine tomorrow.

ALICE

I woke a few days later to my phone ringing – and saw Dad's picture on the screen. He must be on shore again for a day or two if he was video calling. I'd have to warn Willa.

Quickly, I scrambled to sit up and angle my phone so that all he could see behind me was the same blank wall. Then I pressed *Answer*.

"Hi, Dad."

"Hi, Starfish!"

Even thousands of miles away, Dad could still make me smile. "You haven't called me that in years."

"I know. But I saw a particularly beautiful one yesterday morning and it reminded me of you."

"It's still going well, then?"

Lots of enthusiastic nodding. Dad looked tanned, relaxed, happy even.

"But never mind me! How's it going there? In London. And … and with Mabel."

There was something in his voice. Or maybe his face. A hopefulness I hadn't seen before.

"It's fine." I thought back to Willa's texts about the things she'd been doing in London. "Mabel seems ... really nice, actually."

Relief flooded Dad's face. "Oh, I'm so glad you think so, Alice. She is something really special, isn't she?"

Oh no.

Suddenly, the truth hit me. Dad wasn't just trialling Mabel out because he thought I needed a woman's influence. She wasn't just an old friend who'd become something more because I needed a mother. He really liked her.

Maybe even *loved* her.

I'd assumed that Dad had started dating again for *my* benefit. But suddenly, I saw there was a lot more to it.

"She's great," I said, forcing a smile. "So, um, do you expect we'll be seeing a lot of her when you get back?"

Please say no. Please *say no.*

Because if he didn't, all our plans were ruined. We only had another week of the swap left. After that...

"I hope so," Dad said. "But maybe it's something we can talk about when I'm home, yeah? I don't want to rush you into anything."

Which meant there was definitely something to be rushed into.

Now what did I do?

Willa had been *supposed* to be putting Mabel off the idea of being a step-mother altogether – but her texts from London seemed to show them getting on better than I'd imagined. Did I ask her to step up the annoyance factor like we'd planned? Or would that break my dad's heart?

I couldn't do that.

Although if I didn't... Some day, somehow, my dad was going to find out the truth about my summer. And so was Mabel.

What would happen then?

Dad and I chatted for a bit longer, even though my attention was only half on the conversation. The minute he hung up I sent Willa a quick message to update her on everything. Then I lay back on the bed and tried to figure out what to do next.

When there's too many problems to deal with, there's only one thing to do.

I knew Mum's voice wasn't really floating in on the breeze through the window. But I could hear her so clearly in my head. I smiled to myself. One thing I hadn't let go into the flow of the waterfall, after all.

Take one thing at a time. What can you do right now to make something, anything, better?

I couldn't do anything about Dad or Mabel, and Willa hadn't even answered my text yet.

But I was still in Italy, having the summer of my life, with people I cared about. And just for once, I was going to live in the moment and do what I loved.

I was going to go and see the sea.

We'd been planning to go to the beach for the day ever since I arrived in Italy, but there were so many other things to do – around the farm, in the village, not to mention our trek out to the waterfall – that we hadn't made it yet.

Well, maybe today was the day.

Jumping up from the bed, I went to ask Luca and Rosa if they wanted to go to the beach.

Everything else would just have to wait.

WILLA

It was nearly eleven before the party broke up – and I was determined to stay until the end. People congratulated me, or thanked me for my help with their showcase scenes, and I smiled and smiled and took all the praise. I'm not entirely sure what I thought I was proving, but I was definitely going to prove it. I should have been prepping for the audition the next day, but I wasn't thinking about that. Or Hal, or Mabel, or Alice, or anything or anybody except myself.

I'd spent too much time being Alice this summer already. *Willa* would stay and party.

Eventually, Vincent and Billie ushered us all out of the theatre, checking that we all had our phones with us, and a plan for getting safely home. Since mine was supposed to be going home with Hal, I had to come up with a quick lie, but with my acting skills of course they believed me.

Most people's parents had gone out for dinner while we celebrated, then had returned to collect their offspring. They all seemed to disappear into the night before I'd even figured out where I was going. Everything looked different at night.

With Hal already gone, I walked to the Tube on my own, suddenly very aware of how dark the night was, despite the street lights. I'd expected the streets to be empty, but they weren't, and every passing figure made me tense up.

I shouldn't be out here alone, I realized.

I wasn't scared, exactly. OK, fine, maybe I was, a little bit.

I pulled my light summer jacket tight round me, wishing I had the leather one Alice had taken to Italy with her. Even summer evenings in London could get chilly, and it had been a grey day. I looked up at the darkened sky, wondering if it was going to rain – which was why I didn't see the figure approaching from the side until it was too late.

Suddenly, my bag was wrenched from my shoulder, the straps scratching my neck as the thief grabbed it and yanked it away.

"Hey!" I spun round, trying to grab it back, but my hands closed on empty air. They were already halfway down the street before I even thought to follow. I chased them for a few seconds, before realizing that chasing a bag snatcher probably wasn't the best idea, and stopped.

I'd never find them now anyway. My bag – along with my purse, my phone, my keys and my Oyster card – was gone.

I started retracing my steps, trying to stave off the panic that was settling in my chest. I'd head back to the theatre. Maybe Billie and Vincent would still be there, and they could help me.

"I'll be fine," I whispered to myself. "I made it to London this summer on my own. I can figure this out too."

But when I got to the Old Row Theatre, it was in darkness, the doors firmly locked. Now what?

Slow down and take deep breaths. Alice's advice on what to do when freaking out floated into my head.

I wanted to call Hal. Or Alice. Or Mabel. Or even my mum.

I wanted someone else to tell me what to do for once, even though I'd spent my whole summer trying to stop them doing just that.

I didn't have Mabel or Hal's number now my phone was gone, and there was no one else I could call in London. And apart from Alice and Hal – and Billie, sort of – nobody else even knew that Willa

Andrews was in the country.

If I went missing, they wouldn't even know to look for me. They'd be looking for Alice Wright.

That stopped the giggling.

I dropped down to sit on the steps of the theatre, the full horror of my situation sinking in at last.

I wanted Mabel. I wanted to go home.

I don't know how long I sat there before I heard someone ask, "Are you OK, miss?" but it was long enough for me to get chilled to the bone.

I looked up into the face of a policewoman, and almost cried with relief.

"Could you help me get home?"

Riding in a police car through London at night was kind of fun. Finding Mabel waiting up for me wasn't.

"Oh, thank God you're OK," she said, folding me into a hug, as the policewoman left, having explained the situation to Mabel. "I was so worried. And how terrifying! Having your bag snatched in the street like that!"

"I was fine." I wriggled out of her arms. "I was with Hal, but he had to go home a little bit early. But you know, he left me with the other science camp guys."

At that, Mabel stopped, and took a step back, looking at me with raised eyebrows.

"Alice, I called Hal three hours ago looking for you. He said he hadn't seen you since seven thirty. He's been calling every half-hour to check if you're back yet. In fact, I should let him know you're safe."

Even furious with me, Hal had worried about me. Even though I'd lied to him about Alice, and used him all summer to get what I wanted.

"So." Mabel put her phone down and stared at me. "Do you want to tell me where you really were tonight?"

I winced, and looked down at my feet. There were too many lies to unpick and I was running out of energy for coming up with new ones...

Mabel sighed. "I think we should talk about this tomorrow. After we've both had some sleep."

"Mabel, I'm—"

"Bed, Alice," she said, exhaustion in her voice. "We'll talk in the morning."

I woke up late the next day. Washing and dressing quickly, I tiptoed down the stairs – if Mabel was working, I really didn't want to disturb her. I wasn't exactly desperate for our talk.

But when I reached the kitchen there was a note stuck to the fridge that said, 'Gone for a run. Back soon.'

I stared at it for a moment before I realized – this might be my chance to get back into her good books. I checked my watch. Three hours before the audition. Plenty of time to make things right.

I went to grab my purse – before remembering I didn't have one any more. Then I remembered Alice's emergency twenty-pound note, tucked away in the back of her passport holder. If this wasn't an emergency, I didn't know what was, so I tugged it from its hiding place and pulled on my shoes.

Rushing out of the front door of the flat, I went straight to the coffee shop on the corner where Mabel and I had been a few times before.

Armed with a latte for Mabel, and a frozen berry drink for me, plus two huge muffins and two pastries, because I couldn't remember what Mabel liked best – I headed back to the flat, only to pause as I reached the shop below. Flowers. Maybe they'd help too, if I had enough cash left. I'd take all the help I could get right now.

It was a challenge juggling coffee, baked goods *and* the cheapest bunch of flowers they had up the metal staircase again, but I managed it. I was even able to get plates set up and the food laid out before I heard Mabel's key in the lock.

She stood in the kitchen doorway, hot and sweaty in her running gear, and surveyed the breakfast table I'd set out.

"I take it this is an apology?" she said, as I hunted in the cupboards for a vase for the rather sad-looking flowers. "Top right cupboard. Over the toaster."

Vase located, I dumped the flowers in it and turned back to face her. "I'm very, very sorry about last night."

And I was. I felt sorry, and stupid, and most of all guilty. It wasn't a feeling I'd experienced all that often and I *really* didn't like it. I'd been so determined to enjoy myself that I hadn't thought about Mabel. Most of all, I hadn't wanted to admit that Hal had good reasons to be furious with me. I'd screwed up – on all sides.

Mabel nodded slowly, then sighed. "Let me take a quick shower. Then we can talk." She took her coffee with her and headed upstairs.

Fifteen minutes later we sat opposite each other at the kitchen table, me shredding a *pain au raisin*, and her absently picking off bits of blueberry muffin to chew.

"So. Want to tell me what really happened last night?" Mabel said, at last.

I pulled a face. "I'm not completely sure." I'd been thinking about it all morning, and I still didn't know exactly what had made me act so … bratty. Still, I'd managed to come up with a story that fitted all the lies I'd already told Mabel – but was also sort of the truth. "I just … we went to the party with the guys from camp, just like we said we would. But then Hal and I … we kind of got into a fight. And he might have been right, but I didn't want to admit it."

Spelling it out like that, I sounded like a little kid.

"So what happened then?" Mabel asked.

"He walked out. Went home, I guess. I was going to follow, but someone told me to let him calm down first. And then … then I managed to convince myself that it was all his fault anyway, so I insisted on staying at the party and having as much fun as I could … but then I had to travel home on my own and, well, you know what happened next." I wished I'd had a chance to say sorry to Hal. Wished I'd never lied to him about Alice in the first place.

"I hate the idea of you on your own in London

at night too. God, do you know how lucky you were to only lose your bag? If that policewoman hadn't found you…" She shook her head without finishing the thought. I was glad. Just the idea of the possibilities made me shudder. "Your father will be so mad with me."

My head jerked up at that, so I could look her in the eye. "It's not your fault I was stupid!"

"Maybe not," Mabel said. "But I'm responsible for you this summer. So that makes it my fault."

"I'm sorry." My voice came out very small. "I know it was wrong. Dangerous even. And I definitely won't do it again."

Mabel sighed again and reached out to place her hand over mine. "You know, I remember when I was fourteen, my mum told me every day to tidy my room. And every day I ignored her."

"What happened?"

"One day I tripped over a pile of my own stuff and broke my ankle. By the time I got back from having it put in plaster, my mum had bagged up all my stuff and told me that anything I hadn't sorted and put away by the end of the weekend was going in the bin."

I frowned. "Is there a moral or a message I'm

supposed to be getting here?"

Mabel took a huge bite of muffin, chewed and swallowed. "Not really. I just… I guess I didn't do anything very rebellious when I was a teenager. I wasn't that sort of kid."

Just like the real Alice. I bet Mabel's summer would have gone a lot more smoothly if she'd been here instead of me.

"I'm not good at this, Alice," Mabel went on. "I told your dad I wouldn't be, but he said I'd be fine and, well, I wanted to believe him. But when he talked about you… It's like he was describing a different girl. And now you're here, and I don't know how to talk to you and I'm getting it all wrong, and you're staying out until midnight, lying about who you're with and being brought home by the police and I don't know what to do. So I've been thinking about when I was a teenager, and apparently it isn't helping very much."

Guilt swooped down on me, ready to swallow me up.

This was what we'd planned, Alice and I, sitting on that plane. We'd talked about how, after a summer with me, Mabel would hate the idea of ever being a step-mother. How I'd fix it for Alice so she didn't have to worry about Mabel and her dad any more.

And I'd done it – or near enough. So why did I feel so bad?

"It's … it's not you," I said. "I just – this summer is really weird, being away from Dad, being here. And I guess I haven't been handling it very well. But that's not your fault."

Mabel grabbed my hand again, squeezing it tight. "I can't imagine how unsettling it must be for you, being here with someone you barely know. But I'd hoped we'd have time to really get to know each other this summer. To become friends, maybe."

Friends. Mabel didn't want to be another mother like Alice had thought. Mabel wanted to be friends.

"Friends sounds good," I said, with a small smile.

Alice would just have to deal.

"Speaking of friends, do you think there might be someone else you need to make up with too?" Mabel asked.

Hal. Of course.

And I still had an audition to get to. Making up with Hal would be the perfect excuse for me to slope off to the audition without Mabel noticing.

I could do both, right?

I bounced to my feet. "Do you mind if I…" I waved towards the door.

Mabel smiled. "Go. Make up with Hal. But …
dinner together tonight? Just you and me?"

"Definitely. Oh, and could I borrow your phone?
And some money…?"

"Actually, I picked you up this on my run." She
handed me a cheap pay-as-you-go phone, along with
two ten-pound notes. "The phone's already loaded
with credit. So no excuses for not calling if you're
going to be late, or if you need me to come and get
you. OK?"

I smiled ruefully at her. "OK." Then I gave her a big
hug. "Thank you, Mabel."

WILLA

I screwed up. Am making apology rounds now.

WILLA

Also, I had to get a new phone, so this is Willa. In case you hadn't guessed.

WILLA

Lucky for us, my tablet synced all my contacts. Otherwise we'd be in trouble.

WILLA

Well. More trouble.

ALICE

How bad is it? Do I need to start packing?

WILLA

No. Not that bad. Just...

WILLA

I got bratty and made things worse here.

WILLA

Anyway.

WILLA

Have apologized to Mabel with breakfast. Off to find Hal now – well, after my audition.

WILLA

Will fill you in properly tonight.

ALICE

OK. You all right?

WILLA

I'm … not sure, really.

WILLA

I will be, if Hal forgives me.

WILLA

But I need to talk to you about Mabel.

ALICE

Is she being awful?

WILLA

No. That's the problem.

WILLA

She's actually kind of awesome.

WILLA

I think you might really like her. If you ever get the chance to meet her.

ALICE

After this summer? Seems unlikely.

WILLA

Yeah. I guess it does. Talk later x

ALICE

Yeah, later. Off to the beach now!

ALICE

Luca was still feeling bad about his grandparents when I made it downstairs. He said he was fine, but I could tell by the way he was bonding with the donkeys that he was feeling like one of Sofia's lost causes again.

I got Sofia to help me pack a picnic for three, gathered up Rosa, our swimming costumes and some towels, then headed off to drag Luca away from Achilles and Hercules.

"I've got something planned for tonight too – when you three get back," Sofia called after me.

I paused in the doorway and spun round to face her. "What?"

"It's a surprise," was all she would say.

The beach was the perfect place to let go of all the things that were worrying me – Willa's cryptic messages about screwing up, what I was going to do about Dad and Mabel, and what would happen once the summer was over. Even Luca seemed to brighten up when we hit the beach.

I beamed, watching him chase Rosa with a crab. "I knew it. It's impossible to be grumpy by the sea."

"No, it's impossible for *you* to be grumpy by the sea," Luca replied, rolling his eyes at me. Then he got back to chasing his sister, and I knew that whatever he said, this had been the right thing for us all this morning.

"You told me once there were caves here," I said, later, after we'd eaten our picnic. "I'd like to see them. Which way are they?"

I glanced to both sides. To the right, the beach was edged by rocks and grass, leading back inland and to the road that went up to the village. To the left, there were cafés and seafood restaurants and small shacks selling towels and other beach essentials. Further along on both sides, the rocks rose into real cliffs. I guessed one of them held the sea caves.

Luca and Rosa looked at each other, then Luca waved towards the right.

"We can go back the other way for gelato later," Rosa said.

"Sounds like a plan."

The sea caves were cool and damp, with seaweed and shells stuck to the walls and rocks. Dad would love them, I thought absently. Rosa hung back by the entrance, collecting shells, while Luca led me through the network of tunnels and caves, deeper into the cliffs.

Until suddenly I heard what I'd been waiting for.

Falling water. Not as loud as Cascata della Fuga, not even close. More of a trickle than a roar. But still, water, cascading down over rocks from the river above the cliffs. Just like Luca had told me there would be, my first full day in Italy.

"You reckon this waterfall has magic powers too?" Luca asked. He tried to make it sound like a joke, but I wasn't sure it was, not completely.

"Do you really think *any* waterfall has magical powers?" I said disbelievingly.

"No."

"Me neither."

"Really?" Luca gave me an amused look. "Then why did we have to take four buses, walk miles *and* scare off pigs the other day?"

"Because I promised my mum I'd visit that waterfall one day. And because…" I tried to find the words. "It wasn't magic, I know that. But it was cathartic." An English-lesson word that I'd known would be useful one day. "The water didn't take away my worries. I threw them away."

"You definitely seem happier since," Luca admitted. "I don't know how to explain it. It's kind of like … you'd been waiting to say something all summer, and now it's out there."

"I guess it is." Except I'd only told my secrets to the water. Not the people who really needed to hear them.

I could tell Luca now. Spill everything. And I wanted to, I realized. I wanted him to know who I really was.

In the cool damp of that cave, with water trickling down behind us, I wanted him to know *Alice*. Not Willa.

But I couldn't tell him yet. I needed to talk to Willa first. This wasn't just my secret to tell.

"Come on," I said. "We should get back to Rosa."

We spent the rest of the afternoon building a giant mermaid in the sand, complete with seaweed hair and shells for scales on her tail. Luca was strangely obsessive about getting the scales just right, so I left him to it and snapped a few photos of them on my phone instead. I emailed them over to Willa, already a little wistful that my time in Italy was coming to an end. At least I felt like I'd done something worthwhile now, while I was there.

I'd made a real friend in Luca. I just hoped he still wanted my friendship when I finally told him the truth.

WILLA

I retrieved Hal's number from my tablet contacts and texted him from my new phone, asking him to meet me that afternoon. I wanted to do this on his terms, so I picked The Old Operating Theatre as our meeting place. After all, he'd told me that was where he went to think things through. And we both had a lot to think and talk about today.

I just hoped he showed up.

But first, I had an audition to get to.

My nerves were jangling as I made my way across London, though I wasn't sure if it was about my first real shot at an acting career, or worry that Hal might not forgive me. To be honest, the second seemed more important to me – which made me think that pretending to be Alice had rubbed off on me this summer.

I found the building where the audition was being held – which was much harder without my smartphone – and joined a queue of teenagers waiting outside. Slowly, we made our way inside as the doors opened, each checking in at the desk in the lobby.

"Willa Martyn," I said when it was my turn. "The casting director asked to see me personally, after my showcase at the Old Row yesterday."

The person behind the desk just grunted, handed me a number and a sheet of paper, and motioned towards the rows of chairs laid out for waiting.

The whole room was filled with other teenagers – mostly with their parents, in fact – waiting to be called to audition. I saw Tuppence across the room with Ryan and Bethany, but didn't go to join them.

I was too busy thinking.

I should be excited to be here. This was everything I'd been working for all summer. By the end of the day I could have a part on *Heatherside* and a way to keep my dad in my life. Plus I'd have hopefully made up with Hal.

Everything was going exactly to plan.

So why did I feel like I was in the wrong place?

"First time?" the girl next to me asked. She looked a year or two older than me. "You seem nervous," she explained.

I shrugged. "Yeah. First time." I didn't admit to being nervous, though.

The girl stretched out her legs in front of her. "I've done a million of these. They're always the same. You go in there, the people behind the desk barely look at you, you read the script – which they've already heard a hundred times that morning. Then they ask you to do it again, but different, then maybe again … then they send you home. Maybe you get called back, maybe you don't. It's all up to them."

Logically, I knew all this. My parents were actors, after all. But mostly when *they* got called in for auditions it was because the casting director already knew them and wanted them for a role. This – starting out at the bottom – was something different. This was potentially years of auditions, fighting for roles, dealing with rejection – all while also trying to have a normal life, with school and friends and everything.

I had to be honest, it didn't sound as glamorous or as much fun as I'd been imagining.

I'd assumed I'd walk in there and wow them, I realized. But actually, this was my first time auditioning for anything beyond the theatre course at the Old Row. Nobody knew me, or who my parents were, and even if they did they might not care. Maybe I'd get the part, maybe I wouldn't…

But all of a sudden, I wasn't so sure I wanted it.

I frowned, staring down at the script, willing the words to swim back into focus. They didn't. My mind was too busy whirling.

I wanted to talk to Hal, or to Alice, or even to Mabel. Hal would know why I felt this way. Alice would have advice on what to do when I felt nervous and confused. And Mabel would just give me a hug and tell me none of it mattered.

And… I wanted my mum or my dad there with me, like all the others had. I wanted them to tell me stories about their first auditions, the first time they got a part, anything.

I didn't want to be doing this alone.

In fact, I wasn't sure I wanted to be doing it at all.

I'd loved my theatre course at the Old Row, but it wasn't the acting that had made it fun for me. The part I'd loved most was helping the others put their showcases together. I'd liked being the director more than the star.

I didn't want to stand in a room and have other people tell me how to say lines.

I wanted to tell others how to say them.

I blinked. Maybe I didn't want to be an actor at all. And definitely not yet. I had enough people telling me what to do in my life without adding an actual director into the mix.

And it wasn't just that realization that was making me think I was in the wrong place. It was thinking about my parents too.

I'd wanted a part on *Heatherside* at least partly to be closer to my dad – to force him to remember me and make me a part of his life again. He'd run off to Edinburgh with his new girlfriend, chasing a new dream at the Fringe Festival, and forgotten all about me. *Heatherside* had been my way of winning him back.

Except what I'd found in London this summer had me thinking twice. Because here, I had Mabel and Hal. Two people with no real reason to make me a part of their lives – but they had. They'd helped me, looked after me, entertained me, humoured me, worried about me – and I'd repaid them with lie after hurtful lie.

I didn't deserve them. But I knew I needed them in my life.

Mabel... I didn't know what would happen when she learned the truth. Probably I'd never see her again, and that hurt a lot.

But Hal... I still had time to apologize to him, to mend our friendship. A friendship I hadn't realized was so important to me until I'd lost it.

If I had to force my dad to spend time with me when he didn't want to, was it really worth it?

"Hey, where are you going?" the girl next to me asked, as I got to my feet.

"Somewhere more important," I said. Then I left my script and my number on the front desk, and walked right out into the London sunshine, smiling.

This felt right.

Borough Market was bustling when I arrived there. I picked up some gourmet fudge in case my apologies weren't enough, then wound my way through tiny streets, taking the long way round as I thought about what I'd say to Hal, until I reached the Old Operating Theatre. I paid my three pounds fifty to get in, then made my way through the museum to what was apparently Europe's oldest operating theatre. I was early, but I had a feeling that I might not be the only one.

And I was right. There, already sitting in the gallery, staring down at the operating table, was Hal.

"Thinking of chopping off your own leg?" I asked. OK, not my best opener, but I had to say *something*, right?

"I was surprised to get your message." He turned

slowly to look at me. "Don't you have somewhere else to be today?"

"Maybe I figured making things right with you was more important." I handed him the fudge. It looked like we were going to need it.

"More important than your audition?" he said, sceptically.

"Yes, actually." I could have left it there, but I was trying a new thing. Being honest. "But … that's not the whole of it. I went to the audition, then I left before it was my turn."

"Why?"

"I… I decided I don't want the part on *Heatherside*. Or maybe any show."

That seemed to surprise him. "Why not? Wasn't that the whole reason for this ridiculous summer swap thing with … with Alice." He looked down as he said her name, and I realized again how badly I'd hurt him by letting him believe she had feelings for him.

Alice was right. Crushes suck.

Suddenly, the main doors opened and more visitors started pouring in, ready for the historical demonstration. "Come on," Hal said, his mouth full of fudge. "Let's get out of here. You won't like this bit anyway."

Outside, the sun blazed down on the river, and we sat on the wall alongside the Thames and watched the boats pass.

Hal offered the bag of fudge to me and I took a piece. "So why did you decide not to audition?"

I sighed. "Two reasons, really. Firstly... I don't know if you've noticed, but I'm not very good at letting other people tell me what to do."

Hal laughed around his fudge at that one.

"I realized that what I really loved about my theatre course wasn't the acting at all. It was bringing the whole show together. Working with the actors to make their pieces the best they could be."

"I can definitely see you bossing everyone around as a director," Hal agreed. "But you said there were two reasons?"

This was the big one. I twisted the paper bag around the fudge as I searched for the right words. "I guess I... I realized I was doing it for the wrong reasons. I only really wanted the part to make my dad notice me again. But I don't want to chase him for attention any more. He's my *dad*. If he loves me, he should *want* to spend time with me, right?"

"He should. But parents can be rubbish sometimes."

"I know. And neither of mine wanted me around

this summer." I gave him a sideways look. "But you did. You hung out with me this summer, even though you didn't have to. So I figured I'd rather have that sort of friendship than chase after attention from other people."

Hal shook his head. "I don't get it. I mean, I know I was just a convenience to you. An alibi when you needed one. And I know now that you were just stringing me along, pretending that Alice might actually like me when you knew she didn't. I should have known that all along."

"I really *do* think you two would make a great match," I said, and he glared at me. "Really! But I know I shouldn't have led you on like that without checking with Alice first. That was wrong. And I'm really sorry. Mabel told me you texted her every half-hour last night to find out if I was home yet," I said. "You were worried about that, after everything I did?"

Hal shrugged. "I guess I feel a little *responsible* for you somehow. Not because I'd promised Mabel I'd look after you while you were in London, or because I know Alice. Because *you're* my friend, and I wanted you to be safe. That was all."

"Oh." I didn't know what to say to that. "Um,

thank you? And sorry. Again."

Friends. I'd thought I'd had friends before. But none of them had ever felt like the friendships I'd built with Alice and Hal this summer.

We ate fudge in silence for a while. Then, when the bag was gone, Hal said, "I accept your apology."

A weight I didn't know had been sitting on my shoulders suddenly lifted. "Good. Because however this started, we *are* friends, OK? And that matters to me."

"It matters to me too," he admitted.

I tilted my head back and stared up at the blue sky, peeking out between the buildings.

Sitting there with Hal, it was difficult to even remember quite how this summer had started. Alice and I had swapped places, figuring that no one would notice, or care.

They hadn't noticed. But I was pretty sure they were all going to care. Mabel, Aunt Sofia and all the friends Alice had made in Italy. Somehow, while Alice and I were trying to prove a point ... we'd gained new people who cared about us. More importantly, who wanted to help take care of us.

How would Mabel feel when she realized I wasn't the person she thought I was?

A horrible feeling started in my chest and began growing outwards, like the tendrils of some awful plant. The guilt plant.

ALICE

Later, we packed all our things back into our bags and walked along the waterline to buy gelato from a stand on the other side of the beach.

Walking back, I let the waves wash over my feet as I licked my pistachio gelato. Rose had skipped ahead, but Luca walked beside me, the waves barely reaching him.

"Next summer, we should head up to one of the beaches further up the coast," he said suddenly.

I froze, my lips cold against the ice. "Next summer?"

"Well, yeah." He gave me a look – one of those 'Are you crazy?' looks that I was used to from my friends. But not from Luca. "I mean, if we're still staying with Sofia and Mattias, of course. Now you've got to know them, you'll be coming back to visit, yeah?"

"I… Yeah, I guess so."

By next summer, Dad would know the truth, I could feel it. Once he found out, he'd probably never let me out of his sight again.

But Willa … she'd be expected to visit again. Luca

was right. How was *she* going to get around that one? Had she even thought about it? Or just figured that something would show up to work it out?

"We could visit Naples too," Luca went on. "Maybe I could come with Sofia to meet you at the airport in London next time. That would be cool."

"Very cool," I said, my voice faint.

We hadn't thought this through at all, I realized. Neither Willa nor I had thought a moment beyond the end of summer, for all our grand plans.

"I guess my grandparents being useless wasn't the worst thing," Luca said, looking out at the sea, rather than at me. "If it means we get to spend the holidays together again."

"I guess so." My throat felt swollen, in the way it always did before I was about to cry.

Because I wanted that too. But it wasn't mine to have.

I didn't talk much on the way back from the beach. Rosa had Luca playing some weird variation on I-Spy, mostly in Italian, so it wasn't like I had much to add, anyway, despite my lessons with Rosa.

When we reached the farmhouse, there was bunting hanging across the front windows, and tiny fairy lights strung through the olive and bay trees that

Sofia had planted outside. And over the door hung a home-made banner.

One that said: *Benvenuti a Casa.*

Welcome home.

Rosa gasped, and raced forwards to where Sofia was waiting for her in the doorway, and threw her arms round her waist.

"We're staying?" Luca asked, still hanging back a bit. "For good?"

Mattias, standing beside Sofia, nodded. "Your grandparents confirmed it today, and the authorities too. We are officially your long-term foster parents now."

"You're stuck with us," Sofia said, beaming. "And the animals."

"Just as well," I said, trying to keep my smile authentic. "Achilles and Hercules would miss you terribly."

"I've made lasagne," Sofia said, moving aside to let us in. "My traditional homecoming meal."

"Which just happens to be Luca's favourite too," Mattias added.

"And mine!" Rosa said. "Where's Antonio? Can I go and tell him?"

The three of them disappeared into the house. But

Luca stayed outside, staring up at the banner and the lights and the bunting and the whole higgledy-piggledy house.

"Are you glad?" I asked softly. "That you're staying?"

"It just doesn't feel real yet," Luca said. "I mean … everywhere has always been temporary. But long-term fostering … that's the real thing. I guess I thought that this place was too good to be true. That any day now we'd be told it was time to leave again."

I sat down on the stone step in front of the door, and patted the ground beside me until he sat too. "But this afternoon you were talking about next summer."

Luca gave me a sad sort of half-smile. "We always do that. I mean, Antonio used to, when we were little. And now I do it for Rosa. We talk about the place we are now like it's our real home. Like we'll always be there. It helps her not to be so scared." His smile fell away entirely. "Except for when we were places we really didn't want to stay. Then we'd talk about how we'd be home again soon – with Mama, maybe. Or even Dad. Or our grandparents. We didn't remember Dad or Grandma and Granddad so well, but sometimes that made them a better daydream, anyway."

My heart hurt for him, hearing him talk so plainly about his childhood so far.

"Well, I'm glad you get to stay here," I said.

"Because it means we can hang out again next summer for definite?" Luca asked, looking up at me.

I shook my head, glancing away. "Because I think you'll be happy here. And not just until you're eighteen. I think that with Sofia and Mattias ... once you're family, they don't let you go."

We both stared out over the olive groves, towards the village on the hill, the sound of donkeys braying in the background.

This wasn't my place. And it never could be. Especially when they learned that I'd been lying to them all summer.

Unless... Unless I could explain. Make them understand, somehow. Beg for their forgiveness. If *I* told them the truth – rather than them finding out from Willa, or her family ... maybe they could forgive me. Maybe they wouldn't hate me completely.

I needed to talk to Willa. Tonight.

"You know the same goes for you, right?" Luca said suddenly. "I mean, I know you only just met your aunt this summer. But you're family, and

Sofia loves you. She'll always give you a home here, if you need it."

"I hope so," I said quietly. And I'd never meant anything more.

WILLA

Mabel was cooking. Like, actual food.

In the whole time I'd been staying with her, we'd either eaten out, got takeaway, or made sandwiches from stuff she picked up from the deli.

But tonight, she was cooking a real, from scratch, proper meal.

"I didn't know you knew how to do that," I blurted out, as I saw her at the stove.

Mabel flashed me a smile. "I might be making it up a bit as I go along," she admitted. "But I wanted to make you at least *one* home-cooked meal while you were staying with me."

I didn't say that if she was that out of practice at cooking, I'd have preferred another takeaway from the Chinese across the street.

Out in the hallway, a phone rang – the landline, I realized. Weird that she still had one of those, really.

"Can you get that?" Mabel asked, as she poured something into the pan she was stirring constantly.

"Sure." I nipped out and grabbed the phone.

"Hello?"

"Alice?" a voice I'd never heard before said. "Hi, sweetheart. I just tried to Skype you again, but you weren't answering."

Oh God. It was Alice's dad. *Now* what was I supposed to do?

Try to sound like Alice, I supposed. I closed my eyes and tried to hear her voice in my head, then copy it, accent and all.

"Uh, hi. Dad." Oh, that felt really weird. "Um, sorry. I didn't hear it. My laptop's in my room."

"Are you feeling OK, sweetheart? You sound a bit … different from yesterday. Maybe a bit cold-y."

"Probably the pollen from the florist's downstairs," I improvised. "Maybe I'm developing hay fever."

Well, it was a better reason than 'because I'm not your daughter,' anyway.

"Are you sure that's all?"

Oh, he really wasn't buying this. Fooling people who didn't know Alice was one thing. But her actual own father? No way even I could pull this off.

"I'm…" I faked a coughing fit, holding the phone away from my mouth. "Fine," I finished hoarsely. "Just … need water." More coughing.

"Alice?" Mabel asked, coming out into the hallway.

"Are you OK?"

I pointed at my throat and coughed again for good measure. "Need water," I repeated croakily, and handed her the phone before racing for the kitchen.

"I think she's fine, Jon," I heard Mabel saying, as I drank. "Just a frog in her throat. So, how's the data looking today?"

With them safely talking science, I escaped back up to my room until dinner was ready, my heart still racing.

That was too close. It was all getting too close, too real.

And I knew, even before I saw the text from Alice waiting on my phone, that it was time. In fact, I think I'd known since my conversation with Hal that morning – the call from Alice's dad just sealed the deal.

The great summer swap was over.

It was time to tell the truth.

ALICE

OK, you're not talking me out of it this time. We have to tell people the truth.

WILLA

I know.

ALICE

I mean it. Even if you don't, I'm going to. And then you'll have to. If you see what I mean.

WILLA

Alice, I was agreeing with you.

ALICE

Really?

ALICE

I thought I'd have to fight you on this one.

WILLA

Yeah, so did I. But that was before I had to pretend to be you to your dad.

ALICE

You had to do what?!

WILLA

It was fine, I faked a coughing fit and handed the phone to Mabel.

WILLA

The point is, you're right. It's time.

WILLA

But how do we do it?

ALICE

We have to do it at exactly the same time. Otherwise there'll be phone calls and chaos and stuff. So, we need to synchronise watches.

WILLA

We need to do what now?

ALICE

It's just something my dad says. I mean, we need to make sure we get our times right.

ALICE

Let's say we both do it at midday tomorrow – my time. So 11 tomorrow morning for you.

WILLA

That works. Mabel's usually back from her run by then.

ALICE

Great, then. It's a plan.

WILLA

Um.

WILLA

Alice?

WILLA

What happens *after* we tell them?

ALICE

I have absolutely no idea.

ALICE

I felt a strange mixture of relief and anxiety that night when I went to bed – and I still felt exactly the same way when I woke up the next morning.

I hadn't slept particularly well. I'd written in my journal for a while, then it had taken me ages to drop off, and I had all sorts of weird dreams, about Sofia and Willa and Luca and Dad and even a shadowy blond figure I somehow knew was Mabel. None of them made any sense, but there seemed to be a lot of shouting, all the same.

I just hoped it wasn't a premonition.

My nerves were still jangling as I made my way down the stairs to breakfast. Only a few hours to go. Four hours, and the truth would be out – here and in London.

"What's up with you?" Luca asked, as I focused too hard on spreading jam on my roll.

"Nothing." Except that I kept thinking every moment, *This will be the last time I do this*. The last breakfast, the last conversation, the last smile.

Because whatever came after twelve o'clock that afternoon, it wouldn't be the same as before.

I'd never done anything like this before. Never broken the rules. Never jumped without looking. Never acted so completely without a plan.

And I'd loved every moment of it.

OK. Maybe not *every* moment. But if you averaged out all my moments, the results were still pretty stellar.

And I just didn't know what would happen next.

It was … terrifying. But also kind of exhilarating. Freeing, maybe.

Like shouting into a waterfall.

I added more jam to my roll for good measure, and looked slowly around Sofia's kitchen as I committed everything firmly to memory.

The knock on the door made us all jump.

Mattias got up to answer it and, as we waited to see who it was, the nervous, spinning feeling in my stomach grew. It took a moment for me to figure out why.

Mattias was speaking English.

Why would Mattias be speaking English? Unless…

"Willa! Look who is here to see you!"

Too late to run, I froze, my back to the door.

"What, no hug for your dear old dad?"

Scott Andrews. Actor. Willa's father.

What should I do? What would Willa do?

What would *Alice* do next?

My heart pounded in my chest as I realized the truth. There was nothing *to* do, except face up to what I'd already done.

Sofia was on her feet, hugging her long-lost half-brother. Across the table, Luca tried to get my attention, his expression concerned. Even Antonio looked a little confused as to why I wasn't jumping up to greet my father. Rosa just stole another roll while no one was looking.

"Willa?" Sofia said gently.

I was out of time.

Gathering all my courage, I stood up. And then, biting my lip, I turned round to face the man who was not my father.

And that was when all hell broke loose.

WILLA

The tension was too much for me.

I checked the clock on my new phone. Still only 9 a.m. Back in LA I'd probably still be in bed. Here I was rattling around the flat like a restless toddler.

There was only one thing for it. I texted Hal and told him to meet me at the coffee shop on the corner.

"We're going to do it," I said, as soon as he sat down with his mug. "At eleven this morning – midday in Italy – Alice and I are both going to come clean at the exact same time."

Hal's eyebrows shot up over his cappuccino moustache. "You're going to tell Mabel you're not Alice?"

I nodded. "In –" I checked my phone again – "two hours and thirty-seven minutes. You need to keep me occupied until then."

To his credit, Hal did his best. He even confiscated my phone and switched it to silent to stop me checking the time every thirty seconds.

But I couldn't stop thinking about telling Mabel.

Apart from Hal, Mabel was the person who knew me best in this city. Who'd made me welcome in her home and tried to understand and support me, even if I didn't always understand myself.

Mabel was the one I'd betrayed more than anybody. So Mabel deserved the truth.

Eventually Hal gave up on conversation and resorted to screens instead. "Come on. We've got another hour. Let's go back to Mabel's flat and binge watch something trashy and terrible."

"You'd do that for me?" I asked, smiling up at him.

He sighed dramatically. "I'm doing it for me. Even I can't take this waiting any more."

Hal made jokes and teased me about my taste in TV shows all the way back to the flat. Normally I'd have ignored him, but I knew he was only trying to distract me, so I launched a passionate defence of reality TV instead. I was just arguing that observing human nature helps us learn more about ourselves – which definitely sounded like something Alice would say – when I opened the flat door and stumbled through, laughing.

Then I saw Mabel standing at the foot of the stairs, phone in her hand and her face bone white.

ALICE

"Who are *you*?" Willa's dad looked so confused I couldn't help but feel sorry for him.

Sofia looked between us, equally baffled. "Scott? What do you mean...?"

I winced.

Luca got it first. "Oh my God. Who *are* you?"

No magical waterfall could make this go away. Everything in me was screaming to run and hide. To out-race my own embarrassment. To cover my eyes so I couldn't see the disappointment, confusion and anger in the eyes of people who'd been my friends.

Instead, I summoned up every bit of courage I had, sucked in a deep breath and said, "My name is Alice Wright. I'm a friend of Willa's. We met on the plane from LA and, well, we swapped summers, without telling anybody." I met Sofia's gaze and felt like my heart might break. "I'm so sorry for lying to you all. We were... We'd planned to tell everyone the truth today, anyway. Just ... not like this."

Anything would have been better than this. Luca's

expression was stormy, his hands clenched at his sides, and I knew instinctively that I'd have a hard road to win back his trust. I wished I'd just gone with my instincts and told him yesterday, in the caves at the beach. But I'd waited – too long, it turned out.

I tried to catch his eye but he shook his head, backing away. Then, without saying a word, he turned and stormed out.

"Antonio?" Sofia said softly, and that was all he needed. He gathered up Rosa and led her out of the kitchen to follow Luca. I could hear Rosa asking why they had to go – she wanted to stay and listen.

She wanted to stay, and I wanted to go, more than ever.

"You and my daughter … you switched places?" Willa's dad asked incredulously. "Where is she now? Is she OK? Who is she with?"

For someone who'd sent his daughter away for the summer so he could do his own thing, he sounded a lot more panicked than Willa had led me to believe he would.

"She's in London. She's fine. I promise," I said, as soothingly as I could.

"But why? Why on earth would you do such a horrible thing?" Scott asked.

My eyes burned with tears, but I wouldn't let them fall.

"You'll have to ask Willa about her reasons," I said, trying to stay calm. "But I know she was angry about being sent away for the summer to people she'd never met." I turned to Sofia. "I think she'd have loved it if she *had* come, though. I know I have."

"And you, Alice?" Mattias asked, coming to stand behind his wife, one hand on her shoulder for support. "Why did you come here? What was so awful about where you were supposed to be this summer?"

I looked down at the floor, shamefaced. "My dad … he was away for the summer too, working in Australia. We were supposed to spend the holiday together but instead he arranged for me to stay with his new girlfriend in London – a woman I'd never met."

"So my daughter is somewhere in London with some woman nobody knows, getting up to I dread to think what!" Mr Andrews yelled. Apparently he'd gone through disbelief and panic already and landed straight into anger. "I need to speak to Willa. Right now."

"She has her phone," I said softly. "Every time you or her mum have spoken to her this summer, it's really been her. I've been updating her on life here, so she knew what to say." My voice got smaller as I realized the magnitude of our screw-up.

We hadn't just lied to the people we were staying with. We'd lied to our parents too, over and over. And if something had happened to one of us, something worse than Willa getting her bag stolen in London… What would have happened then? How would our real parents even have found out?

Willa's dad stormed out of the room, phone in his hand, punching at the screen with one finger as he went. Quickly, I whipped my phone out of my pocket to text Willa to warn her.

But Sofia was still staring at me, disappointment and betrayal clear in her face.

"I think we'd better call whoever you're supposed to be with right now and explain what's been going on. Don't you?"

I'd never heard her voice so cold. Normally she was all warmth and cheer and happiness. Not today. I'd broken that love and trust she'd given me so freely.

But that was OK. I wasn't her niece, she never had to see me again.

And in the end it was that thought that set the tears flowing.

Sniffing, I dialled the number Dad had given me for Mabel, and handed the phone to Sofia.

It was time for me to go home.

ALICE
Willa, you need to pick up.

ALICE
Your DAD is here.

ALICE
And, unsurprisingly, he's kind of noticed I'm not you.

ALICE
RING ME BACK!

WILLA
Sorry! Hal had my phone.

WILLA
And also TOO LATE.

WILLA

"I just don't understand." Mabel sat at the kitchen table, staring across at me like she was trying to find the answers in my face. "Why would you do something like this? Alice … except that's not your name, is it? You're Willa, right?"

I nodded. What on earth was I supposed to say?

"And you." She glanced up at Hal, standing beside the table. He hadn't been invited to sit, and there were only two chairs, anyway. "You don't seem very surprised. You knew?"

He gave a nod. "I, uh… I've met the real Alice, remember? I knew Willa wasn't her. But—"

"I begged him to go along with it," I broke in. "It wasn't his fault. I told him I'd get him into trouble if he didn't."

Hal gave me a funny look. "No, she didn't. She just … she sounded desperate. And she said that Alice needed my help and, well … I figured if they'd already done the swap, all I could really do was make sure she didn't get into too much trouble."

Trouble. That word was kind of mild for what Alice and I were in right now.

Catastrophic meltdown sounded closer. Although Alice would say I was being melodramatic.

How was she coping, over in Italy, with my family and my *dad* of all people? Dad didn't have the best temper when things weren't going his way...

"You should have come to me, or even your dad," Mabel said, her voice quiet but dangerous. "Told us the truth."

"I know that now," Hal replied, hanging his head in shame. "I'm sorry."

Mabel's attention turned back to me. "And *you*. I don't even know what to say to you. I welcomed you into my home, tried to make sure you were having a great time – and you lied to me from the moment you arrived."

"And that was wrong," I admitted. I never could just leave things there, though. "But..." I started, and Hal groaned.

"No, Hal," Mabel said, her eyes hard. "If *Willa* has an excuse for what she's done, I want to hear it."

"Not an excuse," I said quickly. "An explanation. What we did was wrong, Alice and I know that – that's why we'd planned to tell everyone the truth today, anyway. But the thing is, when we planned the swap, we didn't know you, or my aunt in Italy. Think about it from Alice's point of view, right?"

Now Mabel looked interested. Still mad, but also curious. "OK."

"She thought she was going to have this fantastic summer with her dad, in Australia. Then suddenly she's put on a plane and sent somewhere she doesn't really know, to stay with a woman she's never met, who her dad says is 'an old friend'. *Everybody* knows that means girlfriend." Mabel's mouth twisted a little uncomfortably at that. "But he didn't say that until she asked. He hadn't told her *anything* about you and him dating or anything until he needed to send her here. He didn't *talk* to her about any of it. Not how much you were going to be part of their lives after he got back from Australia, or whether you guys are planning on getting married, or if that'll mean they have to move to London, or *any* of that. So really, can you blame her for not wanting to come here?"

Mabel's mouth opened and then closed again. I glanced up at Hal; he was smirking, just a tiny bit.

"You might be right, there," Mabel said, after a moment. "And what about you? What was so awful about Italy that you wanted to come here instead, Willa?"

I shrugged. "For me ... it wasn't so much not wanting to go to Italy as wanting to be here in London. I ... didn't go to science camp the last couple of weeks. I went to a theatre course instead, one I'd been booked on for *months* before my mum decided to stay in LA."

"*That* was why you came here? A theatre course?" Mabel said incredulously.

"Well, that and not wanting my parents to keep making decisions for me without *talking* to me about them," I admitted.

"Like Jon did with Alice," Mabel murmured.

"*Exactly*. Neither of my parents had time for me this summer, so if they couldn't be bothered taking care of me, I figured it wouldn't much matter to them where I actually went."

Mabel's mouth twitched up into a tiny smile. "I heard your dad in the background when I was talking to your Aunt Sofia, actually. I think it might have mattered to him just a bit."

I could imagine. I just hoped he wasn't yelling at Alice too much.

"So. What happens now?" I asked.

"Sofia and your dad are going to meet us at Heathrow, with Alice, tomorrow. I need to call Jon as soon as it's morning in Australia, fill him in on everything. Except he's out on the boat... Well, as soon as I get to tell him, I imagine he'll be on the first plane home." Mabel sighed and shook her head. "Heaven knows how I'm going to explain all this to him. And when I tell him that I didn't even realize the girl living with me wasn't his daughter, not to mention the lengths Alice went to *not* to spend time with me... Well, I can't imagine Alice is going to have to worry about me being in her life any longer."

A chill settled over me and I shivered. That was the plan – that was what I'd promised Alice I'd achieve for her.

Only now, it didn't feel like such an achievement. It felt like a mistake.

I reached out and grabbed Mabel's hand across the table. "She should. I mean, you should be in her life."

Mabel's smile was sad. "Willa, if the last few weeks – and especially today – have taught me anything, it's that I'm not cut out to be anyone's step-mother."

"No! You've been fantastic. Like when I got my period – which wasn't my first, actually, but I wish it had been!" I saw Hal wince beside me at the mention of periods. I ignored him. "Because you were great. Really great. And I know I haven't always been easy, but you've been kind and understanding, and you've given me my freedom but not *too* much freedom and you've… You've cared. You've taken responsibility for me when you didn't have to, and cared about how I've felt and what I've wanted. You've *talked* to me too, more than my own parents have in *months*." I looked up into her eyes and hoped she was hearing what I was trying to say. "Alice would be lucky to have you as her step-mother. And I'm going to make sure she knows that."

ALICE

I had to wait until Willa's dad stopped shouting at me and turned to shouting at his ex-wife down the phone instead, but eventually I was able to escape and find Luca.

He was with Achilles and Hercules, of course.

"I don't have anything to say to you," Luca said, the minute I appeared at the stable door. He was sitting between the two donkeys, knowing that I still didn't like to get too close to them if I didn't have to. They might not be horses, but I knew they could still pack a huge kick.

But if I wanted to make up with Luca, I'd have to risk it.

"Maybe I have something I need to say to you." I stepped closer, one hand out to pet between Achilles's ears, the way I'd seen Rosa do. "I'm leaving in the morning, as soon as we can get a flight, and I need you to know how sorry I am before I go."

"Fine. You're sorry. That's great. Bye." He still wouldn't look at me.

Cautiously, I sank down to crouch between the donkey's front legs, where Luca couldn't help but see and hear me.

"I made a mistake. I wasn't meant to be here – I should be in London with some woman my dad's apparently dating. But…" How could I find the words for everything that Italy had given me that summer? "But I can't wish we didn't do it because if I hadn't come to Italy, I wouldn't have met you and your family. And if I hadn't met you all, I wouldn't be the Alice I am today."

"And who is that?" Luca asked bitterly. "I thought I knew who you were. I thought you'd been sent away like me. That you'd found a home here like me, because no one anywhere else wanted you. But you've got a whole family out there, haven't you? People who wanted you this summer."

"My dad didn't. We were supposed to be having this brilliant holiday in Australia together, but then suddenly he was sending me to stay with some new girlfriend I'd never met – or even heard of – before." I didn't want Luca's sympathy. But I did want him to know I wasn't a different person now, not really.

"So you had a whole new *family* waiting for you? Not just your dad, but a woman who wanted to be part of your family too? A step-mother, maybe?"

"I… I guess." I hadn't thought of it that way. I'd thought of Mabel as someone pushing in where she didn't belong. Not as someone who wanted to become part of my family to make it better.

"For years, I'd have given anything for just one person who wanted us – *really* wanted to be part of our family. And you had the chance to build a new family and you spat on it. You ran away and you lied."

I couldn't deny it. "I did. And I'm sorry."

"So why did you do it?" Luca asked after a moment.

"Because … because I was avoiding facing reality. Avoiding moving on." I could have claimed I was angry with my dad for sending me away, or for not telling me about Mabel sooner. But I'd had a lot of time to think about my choices while I'd been in Italy, and I knew the real reason I'd agreed to Willa's plan.

The waterfall had cleared away all the things that were clouding my mind – the fear, the pain – until all that was left was the truth. It was time to move on.

Luca shifted slightly, nudging the donkeys apart so I could sit beside him, our backs against the wood of the stable wall. How many conversations had we had, sitting like this, our shoulders pressed together as we talked? The position meant we were unable to see into each other's faces, but somehow that made it easier to talk about the stuff that mattered. The things that came from deep down inside us, that we wouldn't have talked about with anyone else.

How could I have imagined that I'd walk away from Luca, and his family, at the end of the summer and never miss them?

"How did pretending to be someone else help?"

I tried to find a way to make him understand. "My mum died, a few years ago. And since then, it's just been me and dad against the world."

"I'm sorry," Luca said. "But that's not an excuse."

"I know. But… Going to London, meeting Dad's girlfriend … that made it all real. Dad moving on. Mum being truly gone. Which, yes, I knew. But if Dad had fallen in love with someone else that just made it all final, somehow. And doing the sort of things I used to do with Mum, with someone new … that felt like betraying her memory."

And I hadn't been ready to deal with that – or to talk to Dad about how I was feeling.

"So you became Willa instead."

I gave him a half-shrug. "It seemed easier than being Alice, for a while."

"And now?"

"Now it's time to be Alice again."

Luca looked up, finally. "You're more of an Alice than a Willa anyway, I guess."

"I am," I agreed. "But not quite the Alice who got on that flight in LA. A better one, I hope."

"Because of some magic waterfall?"

"Because of you," I said softly. "You and Rosa and Sofia and Mattias and even Antonio. *You* changed me."

"Oh." Luca looked away, seeming embarrassed. "So, what's different about you, then?"

"I think... I *hope* that I'm braver, now. More willing to face up to things. And I think I learned some stuff too," I went on. "About families. How they're not just about blood and birth. They're about the people who love us, whoever they are. Like Sofia and Mattias love you guys. They're your family now, even if it didn't start out that way."

"They're yours too," Luca said. "We all are now."

I shook my head. "Sofia's *Willa's* aunt, not mine."

"But Willa's not the one who's been here this summer, eating gelato and feeding the chickens." Luca twisted to face me. "We might be angry and upset. But that doesn't change the fact that you're one of us now, Alice. You were lost and afraid so you came here. And you know how Sofia feels about scared, abandoned creatures."

For the first time since the knock on the door that morning, a small smile started to spread across my face. Maybe I wouldn't lose the family I'd found here in Italy completely, after all.

WILLA

I shuffled from foot to foot as we stood, staring at the arrivals board at Heathrow. Beside me, Mabel kept glancing from the board to me, as if she was worried I might do a runner.

I probably would have, at the start of the summer. But now I knew it was time to face the music.

We didn't say anything to each other, though. We'd talked a lot the night before, and I guess we were all out of words. What more was there to say except goodbye, anyway?

My dad was meeting us at the airport, getting the same flight as Sofia and Alice, of course. Mum had begged for a break from filming, so she was flying in too. She mostly sounded amazed that I'd been able to keep a secret from her all summer – and that she hadn't noticed I wasn't where I should be when we'd spoken on the phone. Although she did also say that since this had happened on Dad's watch, it should be his job to clean it up – except she didn't trust him to do it right.

Mabel had managed to get hold of Jon on some emergency satellite phone number, and Alice's dad was flying in from Australia, which I guessed was a fairly major thing. Leaving halfway through his research trip probably wasn't going to go down so well with his boss.

But he was coming because Alice needed him. I liked him more for that.

I think Mabel thought it was because he didn't think *she* could handle it, though – especially after she overheard my mum ranting about Dad to me.

I'd texted Alice the night before, telling her about how Mabel had taken the news. How scared she was that she wouldn't be the step-mum Alice needed. I hoped she'd give Mabel a chance, but I didn't know for sure. Alice could be hard to read sometimes. Especially when she only responded with one-word answers.

I wondered if she'd have changed since I saw her. If three weeks of pretending to be me would have made her a different person – the same way pretending to be her had changed me.

Finally the flight landed, and Mabel and I stared at the boards as the status changed. Any time now…

I fiddled with the handle of Alice's case, impatient,

as we waited for them to disembark, collect luggage and all that.

And then, finally, there they were.

Alice spotted me first, then Dad and Sofia. Alice and I exchanged a rueful sort of look as they approached.

I glanced back at Mabel then rushed forwards to meet them – running to Alice, instead of my dad. Alice, being Alice, froze for a second as I threw my arms round her but then she started to relax and hug me back.

"Told you it was crazy," she joked, and I laughed, despite everything.

"Fun, though, right?"

Alice stepped back, and smiled. "It was the best."

Huh. I'd been worried she'd be mad at me – for talking her into the swap in the first place or for how it had all ended. But instead, she looked almost … free. Like she'd relaxed into being herself at last.

It suited her.

I turned my attention to Dad, standing beside my mystery aunt.

Dad's expression had cycled through relieved to angry to resigned to disappointed, all in the time it took him to walk along the rope and reach us. Now, he placed his hands on the sides of my arms and stared down at me, like he was checking he really did have the right daughter this time.

Then he sighed and turned his attention to Mabel. "Thank you for looking after my daughter. I'm sorry she's been such an ... inconvenience."

I stared at my feet, willing myself not to blush. But then Mabel said, "I've loved having Willa to stay with me. She's welcome in my home anytime."

I spun quickly away from my dad and threw my arms round Mabel, hugging her tightly – total opposite to the stiff, awkward hug I'd given her on my arrival, when she'd still thought I was Alice. This hug was all me.

"Thank you," I whispered.

"I mean it," she murmured back. "You'll always have a place in my home."

I turned back to Dad, who took my arm and led me out of the way. "Your mother just texted – she's grabbing her luggage, so should be here any time now. I said we'd meet her in the coffee shop. OK?"

I glanced back at Alice and at Mabel, who both nodded. And as Dad led me over to the coffee shop, I heard Mabel say, "Hello, Alice."

ALICE

"Hello, Alice." Mabel gave me a tentative smile and I tried to return it – but I was thankful for the silent support of Sofia, standing at my left elbow. Really, she should have gone with her half-brother and niece. I couldn't help but feel it meant something that she'd stayed here with me instead.

Maybe Luca was right. Maybe I was one of her lost things.

"Hi," I said back, my voice coming out croaky. There hadn't been a lot of talking on the plane. Willa's dad had just glared out of the window, while Sofia had read her book. They'd kept me sitting between them, though, as if they were afraid I might run off if they gave me half a chance.

"How was your flight?" Mabel asked politely. Close up, she didn't look at all like I'd imagined. Before I spotted her with Willa, the day we arrived, I'd assumed she'd look like Mum, with dark hair like mine and hazel eyes. And since then, I'd tried to put her out of my mind completely, so it was a surprise all over again to see her blond hair, cut to her shoulders. I made myself pay attention, though, to see her as she really was, not as I'd made her out to be in my imagination. She studied me too, with serious green eyes – I guessed looking for all the ways I wasn't Willa.

"It was fine. Um, I'm really sorry about, well, everything." It wasn't much of an apology, but after the last twenty-four hours I was running out of ways to say I was sorry.

Mabel waved aside my apology. "We can talk about that more when your dad arrives. He was hoping to get a seat on the first flight out, but obviously it's still going to take him a while to get here."

My eyes widened. Dad had only managed a very quick call from out on the boat the night before, where I couldn't tell if the silences were because the line was bad or he just didn't know what to say to me. "Wait, he's leaving the research trip? He shouldn't do that. He's waited *years* to get out on that reef."

"That's what I said." Mabel gave me a small smile. "But you know your dad. You're the most important thing in the world to him. And if you've been so unhappy that you needed to run away like this... Well, he's not going to rest until he's checked you're OK and seen you with his own eyes."

"I am," I said quickly. "OK, I mean. And sorry. Sofia and Mattias … they've been wonderful. And their foster children too. I … I was so lucky to be able to stay with them. And I know it wasn't where I was supposed to be, and it was wrong, but I learned a lot while I was there."

I glanced over at Sofia, who gave me an encouraging nod. So I took a deep breath and forced out the sentences that I'd been practising in my head ever since we left Italy.

"I didn't realize… When Dad sent me to stay with you, I didn't know exactly what your relationship was. How Dad felt about you. If things were serious, or if he was just trying to find me a replacement mother. I guess I was kind of hiding from the idea of it. I thought that if I came here, spent time with you – and even liked you, maybe – that I'd be betraying my mother's memory. So I just … avoided the issue. But I know that doesn't make issues go away. And staying with Sofia has taught me that family isn't limited – and neither is love. Letting more people in doesn't push other people – or their memories – out. And I'm sorry it took such extremes for me to learn that. But if you still want to… I'd like to try to get to know you now, please."

Mabel's eyes were wide, her mouth open just a little

in what I assumed was shock. Then she closed it, blinked, and said, "I think I'd like that very much, Alice. We have a day or so before your dad will be back. Maybe we could go to my flat and start again over dinner? I'd like to hear all about your adventures in Italy, for a start."

I grinned. "There was a lot of gelato."

Mabel smiled back. "My favourite. Perhaps we can get some for dessert."

Maybe London wouldn't be so bad, after all.

WILLA

Dad fetched us all coffees, then both my parents stared at me over the table. I took a moment to enjoy seeing them together for the first time in months.

Then I started to get impatient.

"The words you're looking for are: 'I'm so disappointed in you, Willa. I thought I brought you up better than this. Lying to us, to everyone. I can't imagine what you were thinking.'" I'd had enough of Dad's lectures to know the basic form.

But Dad just shook his head, glancing over at Mum. "I *can't* imagine what you were thinking. And that's sad to me, because I used to know how you thought, how you felt about everything. Have we grown so far apart that we can't understand each other at all, any more?"

I shrugged, looking down at my coffee cup. "I don't know. I mean, you're the one who left."

"Is that why you did this? Because your dad and I split up?" Mum asked.

"No." Except it was, a bit. But not the way she meant.

"It's not because you broke up. It's because you walked away, and then so did Mum. Neither of you wanted me at all this summer. You were too busy with your careers and your new girlfriend and your midlife crisis. It's like you both forgot about me completely!"

"That's not true," Dad said. "I could never forget about you. I thought about you every day."

"You just didn't want to have to do more than think. You didn't want to actually have to deal with the reality of me being there every day."

That made him pause, and this time it was *him* staring guiltily into his coffee cup.

"I thought... I wanted to do my theatre course, in London. You'd promised me I could, Mum. And Dad, you said it would be fine because you'd be working those afternoons in London anyway. It was all *planned*."

"*That's* what this was about?" Dad asked. "Some stupid drama course?"

"It *wasn't* stupid!" I could feel tears pricking behind my eyes, but I wasn't going to let them fall. "It was important to me, and you knew it."

"It was just a summer course," Mum said, talking to Dad rather than me. "Nothing special."

"It *was* special. Because the *Heatherside* casting agent

was there for the showcase, and if she liked us we got invited to audition for the new family they're adding to the show. And if I got the part I'd have been able to see Dad every single day we were filming, even if you two never spoke to each other again." I might have given that dream up, realizing it wasn't really what I wanted. And knowing that if I had to force my dad to spend time with me it wasn't worth it. But it still hurt to think of the lengths I'd had to go to in order to get their attention.

Silence greeted my outburst. So I figured I might as well fill it.

Calmer now, I said, "At least I know I made a mistake. I thought about myself first and other people, well, not at all, really. I did the wrong thing, I lied and I cheated and I'm sorry about it," I went on. "You two … you won't even admit you've done anything wrong."

Mum and Dad exchanged a long look.

"You wanted to see your dad?" Mum asked. "Why didn't you just tell me that?"

"Because you were so angry with him," I replied. "And it was all about us girls making a new life together. How could I tell you how much I missed him after what he'd done?"

"We *were* wrong," Dad said, after a long, heavy moment. "I know I handled things badly, with the break-up. But we shouldn't have put our problems above your happiness."

"We should have planned for this summer better," Mum agreed. "Made sure one of us was there to spend time with you. But everything's been so ... difficult between us since your father left."

"I noticed," I muttered.

"I'm sorry, Willa. Really I am." Dad reached across the table and took my hand. "We never meant for you to get caught in the middle like this. And I *did* miss you – that's why I flew to Italy in the first place. I wanted to surprise you all."

"Yeah, well." Apologies were all well and good. But how were they going to make anything different?

"So ... did you make the audition?" Mum asked. "Not that it matters of course – except that it matters to you, so..."

"I did," I replied. "But... I didn't go. I realized that, as much as I like acting, I don't think I like it enough to do it as a job already. In fact, I was thinking I might prefer directing."

Mum and Dad exchanged an amused look. "I can definitely see that," Mum said.

It was nice to see them smiling at each other again, for the first time in months – even if it only lasted a few seconds. But then, just when I thought we were going to go back to awkward silence, Dad jumped to his feet.

"Let's go to LA, right now. All three of us."

"What?" Mum and I said together.

"You need to get back for filming, right?" Dad said to Mum. "Well, I'll come too. Spend time with Willa while you're working. The festival's over, so I've got a bit of a break now until I go back to *Heatherside* next month, and Willa will have to go back to school before then anyway. But we'll have a week or so. And when you're not working, we'll sit down, the three of us, and figure all this out together. How we're going to manage the holidays, and the rest of the year, so that everyone is happy. I never want to go so long without seeing my girl again. OK?"

Mum nodded, looking slightly shell-shocked. I wondered briefly where Dad would be staying while all this happened. The apartment Mum had rented for us only had two bedrooms, and the sofa wasn't very comfortable.

But worrying about the logistics was an Alice thing to do. I was going to focus on the big picture instead.

Both my parents, in the same room, talking amicably about how to make my life better – and actually including me in the conversation? It seemed as likely as them buying me a unicorn for Christmas, but if they were willing to try I definitely wasn't going to say no.

I grabbed my case and stood up. Wait … suitcases.

"I just need to go swap my stuff back with Alice," I said. Then another thought occurred to me. "And actually, I need a word with Sofia and Mabel before we start our negotiations too."

Yep, I was definitely all Willa again. And Willa Andrews always found a way to get what she wanted.

This summer would be no exception.

ALICE

Mabel and Sofia hit it off instantly. I probably shouldn't have been surprised. They were still chatting about the Italian coastline when Willa and her dad came back from the coffee shop. Willa was dragging my suitcase behind her, and she had a scarily determined look in her eye.

Last time I saw that look, I'd ended up being Willa Andrews for three weeks. I was almost afraid to ask what she had planned this time.

"We still need to swap our stuff back," she said, as she approached.

"Are there any of my clothes left in there?" I joked.

Willa shrugged. "I might have burned the five-year-old's party dress. But I promise I replaced it with *much* better stuff."

I wasn't going to complain. I'd actually grown used to Willa's style over the last few weeks.

Flipping open Willa's case, I pulled out the bag of my stuff I wanted to hold on to from my Italian adventure: a notebook I'd bought from the little stationer's in the village, a recipe for Sofia's grandma's lemon cake, a bottle of Mattias's olive oil for Dad, that sort of thing.

Willa did the same, though not as neatly. I'd organized the stuff I wanted to keep into one bag, but it looked like Willa hadn't thought about the swap until this moment, so she basically unpacked all my clothes – and quite a few I didn't recognize – on to the floor of the airport terminal, then shoved them all back in again once she'd rescued her stuff.

"Your dad told me how neat and tidy you liked things," Mabel observed as we watched Willa's performance. "I assumed you were being messy because you didn't like me. Turns out, that's just Willa."

"Sorry," I said, for what had to be the hundredth time.

Mabel shrugged. "I should have figured it out sooner, was all I was thinking."

"For what it's worth, I'm kind of glad you didn't," I said. "I think we'll have a nicer visit now."

"Me too," said Mabel.

Willa zipped up my suitcase again and wheeled it over to me. "So."

"So," I echoed.

"We should really do this again sometime," Willa

said, her eyes dancing with mischief.

I couldn't help it. I burst out laughing.

"No, I mean it!" Willa spun me round so we were both facing the adults. "Alice and I have been thinking. We really have become friends this summer – and we've both made friends in London and Italy too. We'd hate to never see them – or each other – again."

Willa's dad exchanged a look with Mabel and Sofia. "So, what were you thinking?"

"I'm so glad you asked!" Willa said lightly, but I knew she wasn't joking. Being asked what *she* wanted for a change was one of the things this summer had been about. "I think that next summer, Alice and I should get to holiday together. A week in Italy with Aunt Sofia, and another week in London with Mabel and Alice's dad. What do you think?"

"You didn't ask *me* what I wanted," I muttered to Willa as the grown-ups huddled to discuss.

"Did I need to?" Willa asked. "I figured that after being you for three weeks I knew what you wanted – the same as I do. Right?"

I thought about a week in Italy with Luca and the others, but this time as myself, and with Willa along too to join in the fun. And then I considered having her to keep me company in London if I had to stay with Mabel.

"Yeah, OK. You were right."

"I knew it!" Willa beamed with satisfaction. "And maybe you can even come out to LA and stay before then, if you'd like?"

"Sounds brilliant."

The grown-ups separated again and turned to look at us.

"Well?" Willa asked.

"I'll need to talk to Alice's dad," Mabel warned.

"And we'll need to factor it into our discussions about holidays," Willa's dad added, while her mum nodded along.

"But since you'll probably just figure out some other way to make it happen if we don't agree," Sofia said, grinning, "I think it sounds like a great idea."

"Yes!" Willa threw her arms round my shoulders and we hugged each other tightly.

I felt like I was back at Cascata della Fuga once more. I'd see Luca again. And Rosa and Antonio and Mattias and Sofia and Achilles and Hercules and even the chickens.

Most of all, I'd get to keep the friendship I'd built with Willa.

And maybe I even had the chance of building a new relationship with Mabel. Not with her as my mother, but as another part of my family.

If my summer swap had taught me anything, it was that family could be found anywhere – and you could never have too much of it.

Mine had definitely grown this summer. And I couldn't be happier about it.

WILLA

Good luck with your dad tomorrow.

ALICE

Thanks. And good luck with your negotiations with your parents.

ALICE

Let me know how it goes.

WILLA

Will do. You too.

WILLA

We need to start making plans for the holidays...

ALICE

Definitely!

WILLA

I was thinking, do you reckon if we told Mabel we were in Italy and Sofia that we were in London, anyone would notice if we skipped off to Disneyland Paris for a week next summer...?

Acknowledgements

Any book I write is always the result of a huge amount of support from others – all of whom have my heartfelt thanks. For *The Switch Up*, I'd particularly like to thank:

• My agent, Gemma Cooper, for not laughing when I said, 'Okay, so, new idea: two fourteen year olds meet at an airport and swap lives for the summer'

• My publisher, Stripes, and everyone there who has worked so hard to make this book a reality, including the people below (but not limited to, because I'm bound to forget someone! If it's you, I'm really sorry and I love you really)

• The fantastic editors who worked on this book with me; Rachel Boden, Emma Young, Ella Whiddett and the always awesome Ruth Bennett

• Paul Coomey and Sara Mognol for designing a cover I absolutely adore

• Leilah Skelton, Lauren Ace and Charlie Morris, for getting the book out into the world and into readers' hands through great publicity and marketing strategies

• Elle Waddington for taking the book overseas and finding even more new readers through foreign rights deals

- Team Cooper, always, for support, love, and amazing advice at all hours
- My husband, Simon, for simply being the best person anyone ever married
- My daughter, Holly, for being my first reader and laughing in all the right places
- My son, Sam, for cuddles at vital moments, and putting up with pasta and pesto for dinner every night when I'm on a deadline
- The Cannon Family Singers, for constant WhatsApp entertainment. Also for being incredible parents and brothers
- All the Cannons, Watsons, Reeveses, Whitleys, Nichols, McAleavys, Quigleys, Freemans and Woods, for showing me what true family means and why it matters so much
- My incredible friends, for demonstrating daily what great friendship looks like, and how to support the people we love. Thank you all for loving and supporting me, always. Also for the tea, cake, spreadsheets and takeaway curry
- My wonderful readers – especially every single person who messaged or emailed to ask when my next book was coming out. I love knowing you're as excited for my stories as I am. I hope it was worth waiting for!